CHRISTMAS AT DEVIL'S GATE

Miss Honour Fitzroy is fleeing from her cousin, Sir Edward Fitzroy, who is trying to force her into marrying his son in order to gain access to her fortune. When her carriage breaks an axle in the snow, she takes refuge at a house she believes is called Devil's Gate. There she encounters Major Ralph Duval, who develops a fondness for her and vows to protect her from her cousin. Will Ralph be able to keep her safe, or will Sir Edward's plan succeed?

D1578529

FENELLA J. MILLER

CHRISTMAS AT DEVIL'S GATE

Complete and Unabridged

LINFORD
Leicester

First published in Great Britain in 2017

First Linford Edition
published 2019

A catalogue record for this book is available
from the British Library.

ISBN 978–1–4448–4099–5

Published by
F. A. Thorpe (Publishing)
Anstey, Leicestershire

Set by Words & Graphics Ltd.
Anstey, Leicestershire
Printed and bound in Great Britain by
T. J. International Ltd., Padstow, Cornwall

This book is printed on acid-free paper

1

The carriage had ice on the inside of the window. Honour huddled under the furs and wished for the umpteenth time she had not been forced to flee Cousin Edward's house whilst the weather was so appalling.

'Sally, if you don't stop crying this minute I shall kick you.' This was hardly an encouraging statement or indeed the sort of threat a young lady should make to her maid, but they were more friends than employee and servant as they had been together since they were children.

The shivering girl sniffed loudly. 'You go ahead, miss, I don't reckon I'd feel it as my limbs are frozen solid.'

'If you would only come and sit next to me as I requested we would have double the amount of rugs and be able to share our body heat. Do not dare to say that it's inappropriate behaviour. I am as cold as you and this is one way we can get warmer.'

Their breath steamed in front of them and she couldn't feel her fingers let alone her toes. Reluctantly Sally gathered her rugs and stood up. It was unfortunate that at the very moment she chose to do so the rear wheel dropped into a frozen rut. The carriage lurched sideways and the girl fell heavily against the side that was already tilted. What happened next was inevitable.

Honour was thrown on top of her maid as the rear axle snapped and the vehicle slowly toppled onto its side. For a moment she was winded but soon recovered.

'Are you hurt?'

'I am not, miss, but I'd be a sight better if you were not crushing the life out of me.'

The horses were panicking and she could not hear the coachman or under-coachman tending to them. 'I'm going to attempt to get out of the door. You will have to roll to one side to allow me to reach the handle. At the moment we are both on top of it but the carriage isn't quite flat. I think there might be room for me to wriggle through the gap.'

This manoeuvre was successfully completed and she was able to push the door open sufficiently for her to crawl through. Sally immediately did the same and together they slithered on their bellies from under the coach until they were able to stand.

'See what has happened to the men whilst I calm the horses.'

The snow was up to her knees, small wonder the carriage had come to grief. John Coachman should have pulled in at the last hostelry and not continued along this deserted country lane. Thank God they were both wearing stout boots and their warmest clothes. She had her riding breeches on under her cloak and gown which meant she was better protected than her companion.

She waded to the horses and grabbed the bit of the one nearest to her. 'That's enough, Peggy, you will break a leg if you continue to misbehave.' The mare immediately responded to her voice and touch and stopped plunging. Sultan, the matched grey gelding, nudged her with his nose. Both animals were pleased to see her.

The traces were entangled around their legs and they were fortunate not to have come to grief. She was well used to harnessing a team and deftly removed both of them from the twisted leather and led them to a safe place away from the ruined carriage.

The horses would suffer if they were outside in these inclement conditions for much longer. Always see to your horse before you see to your own comfort, was what her dear departed father had always said to her. If only Papa had not died so suddenly she would not be in this predicament.

Why was Sally so quiet? A sick dread settled in her stomach. She turned to see her maid, ashen-faced, staring down at two ominously still shapes in the snow.

'Is there nothing we can do?'

'They must have broken their necks in the fall. I've never seen the like — for two men to die so suddenly and without a sound.'

'I'm going to drape the rugs over the horses, you do the same with the cadavers. We cannot remain out here and survive. It will be dark in an hour or two and the temperature is falling.'

'What about your trunks, miss?'

'They will have to take their chance. I think it unlikely foot pads or brigands will be out looking for victims today. We have my jewellery and other valuables safely hidden beneath our skirts — the other things can easily be replaced if needs be.'

The horses waited patiently, warmer now they were covered with the furs, and seemed content for them to scramble up onto their backs. Sally was an indifferent horsewoman but Honour was sure the girl could stay on board if her life depended on it, which in this instance it might well do. As for herself, she preferred to ride bareback and astride when the opportunity presented itself.

'There is little point in going back as we are more than two hours from the last inn. We must pray that there is a house close by we can take refuge in until the weather clears.'

'At least it isn't snowing now, we must be thankful for small mercies, Miss Fitzroy.'

Peggy responded to her kick and moved off willingly, Sultan followed as he always did. The horses were up to their hocks in snow. If they didn't find somewhere to shelter soon they would all perish. The wind was bitter, even with her hood pulled down and her muffler tied tightly around her face, she was still scarcely able to breathe.

Then on her right she saw a pair of imposing gates. Her heart skipped and then plummeted again. They were bolted from the inside and there was no gatehouse. There was something written on the wrought iron arch that spanned the drive. It was partially obscured by the snow. She strained to read the words and was almost sure it read *Devil's Gate.* Surely that couldn't be right? There was no time to dwell on this. She needed to climb the gate, devil or not, and push back the bolts.

'Here, hold onto Peggy. I'm going to stand on her back and then go over and let us in.'

'I'll do it, I was always better climbing trees than you, miss.'

This was undoubtedly true but she was determined to be the one who took the risks. Sally was under her protection so it must be she who attempted the dangerous ascent.

'You will do as you're told for once. I have better balance than you, anyway.' Not waiting for a reply, time was of the essence, she gripped hold of the icy iron to steady herself and then began to scramble up. The cold seeped through her gloves, her fingers slipped and when she was swinging her leg over the top she lost her toehold and tumbled over the gate.

Sally screamed and continued to do

so, the hideous sound echoed beneath the overhanging trees.

Honour thought her last moment had come but by some miracle her cloak had become entangled with the finial on top and saved her from a possibly fatal fall. Once she had recovered from the shock she scrabbled with her toes and managed to steady herself.

'Enough, Sally, I'm not dead and if you continue to make that racket you will spook the horses.'

The screaming stopped. 'I thought you were going to die and that I would be alone out here.'

'Well, as you see, I am not hurt, merely stuck.'

* * *

'My lord, I'm sure Desdemona will whelp without your assistance, there's no necessity for you to go out yourself.' Gifford, his valet, said urgently.

Ralph ignored his man as he usually did. 'I shall not be long, there's no need

8

to fuss like an old woman.'

'You are not fully recovered from your injuries, sir; Doctor Fulbright was quite clear on this subject. You are to remain inside and rest until he returns in the new year after your fever last week.'

'He's another old woman. I'm perfectly capable of going out to the stables. I don't trust the new kennelman; I want to be certain my bitch doesn't perish through lack of attention.'

Gifford and Fulbright didn't know how mouldering inside was destroying his health, not aiding his recovery. The sabre thrust he had received from a French cavalry officer should have proved fatal, but somehow he had survived and managed to return to recuperate at his ancestral home. If the wound in his side had festered he would have died, only the skill of the army surgeon had prevented this.

He was determined to rejoin his regiment in the spring and refused to resign his commission. His command, the finest men in Wellington's army in his opinion, needed him to lead them into the next battle if they were to survive. The fact that he was the last of his line meant nothing to him. As far as he was concerned the Duval family were cursed and he had no intention of marrying and producing an heir to inherit the crumbling house and estate. Far better to die an honourable death, unlike his ancestors, fighting for King and Country.

He kept only half a dozen servants, none of them female, and most of the house was under holland covers. He lived in the downstairs apartment, he'd not been into any of the bedchambers since he was a stripling. They had been the scene of debauchery, drunkenness and gambling. His poor mama had died from shame when he was still away at school. His older brother had followed in their father's disreputable footsteps.

He pulled up the collar of his greatcoat and stepped out onto the flagstone path that led directly to the stables where his favourite hound was in the process of producing a litter. These dogs were in high demand and a vital source of income. Indeed, if it weren't for the dogs and his pay as a major, he would be more or less destitute.

He was halfway to his destination when he heard a woman's scream. The sound sent shivers down his spine reminding him of the atrocities he had inadvertently witnessed in this very house.

Without conscious thought he set off at the double towards the noise. It was half a mile to the gates and they were hidden until he rounded the curve in the drive. The screaming stopped as the gates came into view.

He almost fell over his feet at what met his eyes. Dangling from the top of the closed gates was a young lady — on the other side were two handsome greys and a second girl. He increased his pace and arrived not a moment too soon.

11

There was the sound of tearing material and with a despairing cry the girl on this side tumbled into his arms.

He broke her fall, which was good, but his left leg gave way and they both went sprawling into the snow. She recovered first and instead of berating him she spoke from beside him. 'I have hurt you, I beg your pardon, I should have hung on longer and made a less precipitous descent.'

As the pain receded he was able to breathe normally again and opened his eyes. Staring down at him was the face of an angel. Golden hair framed a heart-shaped face and the prettiest sky-blue eyes he had ever seen. He forgot what he had been going to say and said something else entirely.

'Will you marry me?' Her look of astonishment made him smile. 'I beg your pardon. I had better introduce myself before you answer.' With some difficulty he pushed himself upright; they were still both sitting in the snow. He stretched out and grabbed hold of the gate in order to haul himself upright. She was about to offer her assistance but thought better of it when he frowned.

'To continue, I am Major Ralph Duval. And you are?'

She rose gracefully and shook the worst of the snow from her ruined cloak. 'I am Miss Fitzroy. I've no time for your nonsense, sir, I need to get the gate open and my horses and maid into shelter before they freeze to death.'

Rudely she turned her back on him and without apparent difficulty managed to loosen the bolts and slide them across thus allowing the gate to open. Fortunately, the snow had not settled on this side as deeply as it had on the other and she was able to pull it wide enough for the two horses to enter single file.

He was feeling decidedly odd, he feared he had reopened his wound. There was certainly a clammy wetness where the stitches had been placed months ago. He was only remaining on his feet by hanging onto the gate. From a distance he heard the girl talking but couldn't make sense of what she said. Then the all-too-familiar blackness washed over him and he knew nothing else.

★ ★ ★

'Quickly, Sally, he's about to swoon. Help me to support him so we can get him across one of the horses. We won't be able to lift him once he is on the ground — he's a prodigiously large man.'

Together they managed to push him over the pommel and Peggy was so cold and miserable she didn't object to this unaccustomed load.

'I'll mount Sultan first and then you must scramble on behind me. We need to get him back to the house immediately.'

The drive was long and cold and by the time they were in sight of the building snow had started to fall again and they could barely see a yard in front of their faces. Someone in the house must have been waiting for their approach as they were still a distance away when a group of servants hurried towards them.

'Thank God, your master is unconscious. He was attempting to help me and I fell on top of him. Has the major been recently injured?'

The tallest man, also muffled in a thick greatcoat like the others, took the lead rein from her. 'His lordship was grievously hurt several months ago and not thought to survive. His physician was most insistent that he remain inside after his recent fever, but he would go out to attend to his hound who is whelping.'

'That is something I know about. I am proficient at doctoring people, but expert when it comes to horses and dogs. Sally, my maid, is as good as any doctor. She shall go with you and do what is needed to help, I shall find the bitch and do what I can to assist her

15

with her puppies.'

The stables were blissfully warm, several equine heads turned as she entered with her own mount, and she spoke soothingly to them. A grizzled groom shuffled in and touched his cap. 'I'll be doing for this one, and the other when it comes, you get on in and get warm, missy.'

'I've come to oversee the puppies' arrival. I take it they are in the end stall as that is where the whining is coming from?'

He grunted and left her to it. A servant didn't argue with his betters if he intended to remain in his employment. The bitch was slick with sweat and obviously in distress. There were no puppies in the straw next to her — something was seriously wrong with this delivery.

She removed the remnants of her cloak and her gloves and then knelt beside the hound. 'Lie still, sweetheart, I'm going to help you deliver these pups.'

The first of the litter had become wedged inside, it took but seconds to straighten it and pull it free. It lay limp on the straw but she wasn't about to give up so easily. She picked it up, cleared its mouth and nose of matter and then swung it around a couple of times by its back feet.

Whilst she attended to this first arrival she kept an eye on the mother but the dog was now progressing smoothly without the need for her interference. She rubbed the limp puppy vigorously and was rewarded by a small movement. He was alive. The rest was up to his mother — the bitch's tongue would do more good than she ever could.

Gently she put the firstborn next to his mother and immediately the hound licked it. She did the same for each puppy and within an hour there were nine suckling happily. Honour had been so involved in what she was doing she was shocked to find she had an admiring audience when she eventually

17

stood up to stretch her legs.

'That were well done, Miss Fitzroy, his lordship will be that pleased you delivered all of them safely. Them little'uns are worth a small fortune.'

'I shall leave you to clean the stall and make sure the mother has fresh water and something to eat. Do not hesitate to send for me if there is any cause for concern with that one.' She touched the largest of the puppies that had almost died at birth.

'I reckon he'll do now. Look at the little blighter feeding like a good'un.'

'Then I'll go to the house if someone would be kind enough to direct me.'

A slightly younger and smarter man stepped forward and bowed which seemed strange considering the circumstances. 'I was sent to conduct you to your chamber, Miss Fitzroy, if you would care to follow me.'

There was little point in putting the cloak back on, so she would have to brave the elements as she was and hope she did not freeze to the marrow before she got inside the house.

'Here, miss, the master says as you would need this.' The young man held out a thick greatcoat and she stepped into it. She inhaled and caught a mix of lemon soap and something more masculine. This belonged to the major, she supposed she must call him Lord Duval.

In her experience aristocrats were no better than anyone else and she had no intention of treating him as if he were a demigod just because he held a title he had inherited.

She smiled wryly as she pulled his coat tight around her body. The house was called Duval's Gate not Devil's Gate. An easy mistake to make in the circumstances and she sincerely hoped it was not prophetic. Being stranded in the house of a stranger, in the middle of nowhere, in the worst storm of the winter could well cause problems for her in the future.

She had only embarked on this foolhardy journey to escape the machinations of her cousin who intended that she marry his unpleasant son so he could get hold of her inheritance. She straightened her shoulders and stepped out into the bitter cold determined that, come what may, she would never marry Robert. She would rather marry the devil himself than him.

2

Ralph came around as an unknown girl was stitching him up. He knew better than to move whilst this delicate operation was being done. She was remarkably efficient and the pain wasn't as excruciating as it might have been.

He kept his eyes closed until the procedure was completed and then swallowed gratefully when she held a jug of watered wine to his lips.

'Your scar tore open, my lord, but it's not too serious. You lost a fair amount of blood, but if you rest in bed and drink plenty of this, you will be fighting fit in time to celebrate the birthday of the Lord.'

'As that is not for a further two weeks, I sincerely hope you are right. Thank you for your able doctoring. I think I might well owe my life to you.'

'Only fair that I put things right

when it was my mistress who caused the damage.'

He drained the jug and although the wine was diluted he was unused to alcohol of any sort and he drifted off to sleep in a pleasant alcoholic haze.

The next time he awoke he thought he was alone. There were no candles lit but there was sufficient light from the fire crackling in the grate for him to see perfectly well. Having consumed so much liquid he had an urgent need that could only be met by getting out of bed and he doubted he was strong enough to do that on his own.

There was a small brass bell beside the bed and he stretched out to ring it.

'I expect you need to relieve yourself, my lord. I have a suitable receptacle here, there is no need for you to get out.'

'I shall not get out, miss, but you will. Have you lost your wits to be alone in a gentleman's bedchamber in the middle of the night?'

'As you were comatose until a

moment ago I don't believe I was in any danger of being ravished.' The girl handed him the necessary item. 'However, I shall now go to my bed. Your man will be with you directly and take care of any other needs. Good night, my lord.' She moved out of his line of vision but then drifted back. 'By the way, your hound has nine healthy puppies.'

How the devil did she know that?

★ ★ ★

Gifford remained with him for the rest of the night and by morning Ralph felt so much better he was determined to get up and go and see the new litter for himself. There was already a waiting list for the puppies and the sale of them would bring a welcome boost to his finances.

'Fetch me something to wear, I intend to get dressed.'

This time it wasn't his valet who answered but the interfering girl. 'You will do no such thing. I have given your man instructions to remove all your garments from your reach. You must remain where you are for at least another day if you do not want your wound to open for a third time.'

He muttered something extremely impolite under his breath and she tutted like an old maid.

'Kindly keep your barrack-room language to yourself, my lord. Now, if you agree to remain where you are I shall allow you to have a more substantial breakfast than you would get otherwise.'

This was too much. 'I will not be dictated to by anyone, and especially not by a chit scarcely out of the schoolroom who has somehow insinuated herself into my household without my permission. Did I not tell you last night to remove yourself from my bedchamber?'

She was unmoved by his tirade. 'I believe that you did, but as you can see I have ignored your wishes.' Her teasing tone changed and she moved closer and he could see genuine distress on her face. 'You are only in this state because of me. You came to help me and I fell and injured you. I do most humbly apologise for doing so.'

'I accept your apology. However, I insist that you leave immediately. Tarnation take it! Are you so naïve that you don't know the significance of your being here?'

'If you are suggesting that somehow you have compromised me and must offer to marry me, then you are sadly mistaken, sir. My reputation is my own concern and I can assure you that it will not be damaged by anything that happens here. How could anyone in Society even know that I am residing temporarily under your roof?'

He flopped back on the pillows. '*Touché*, my dear. I have remained incommunicado since I returned from the Peninsular and I doubt that any of my neighbours are aware I am here. I have yet to learn what you were doing hanging from my gate yesterday?'

'I was climbing over so I could open it, I thought that would have been obvious to a man of your intelligence.'

She was prevaricating, but he was determined to get to the truth. 'I must surmise that you were running away from someone or something. Tell me, which of these is it?'

'I suppose I owe you an explanation. I am an orphan, unfortunately my obnoxious cousin, Sir Edward Fitzroy, is my legal guardian. He is determined to marry me to his equally obnoxious son in order to get access to my considerable fortune. I am equally determined that he shall not do so.'

'I thought it must be something of the sort. How old are you?'

'I shall be one and twenty on New Year's Day and will then have access to my funds and be free of both of them. If I can remain out of their clutches until then I shall be safe.'

'The weather is abysmal, I doubt the snow will clear before the festive period ends. So even if you intend to leave you cannot do so. Presumably you were not travelling on horseback?'

Her expression changed and she blinked furiously. 'My coachman and his assistant were both killed in the accident. My belongings remain in the carriage about half a mile from here.'

'Ring that bell for me, I'll get my men to use the sledge and fetch your trunks and take care of the corpses. They can be buried in the family graveyard but there will be no mealy-mouthed clergyman attending the service. I doubt anyone will have stolen your things yet.'

'I have no wish to be a nuisance, I've caused more than enough damage already. As long as they are both treated with reverence, I shall be content.' She curtsied and he nodded politely. She then changed the subject and continued the conversation as if they had not been talking about her dead servants.

'I should be honoured to be allowed to remain here until after my name day. Do you have exciting plans in place for Christmas?'

Gifford appeared and Ralph quickly gave his orders. The man vanished to take care of things. Gifford had been with him since he had bought his colours many years ago. He was more like a brother than an employee.

'To return to your previous question about my festive plans. I have none. As far as I'm concerned one day is exactly like another. My staff are free to do as they please, if you feel the need to make merry then you have my permission to join them in the servants' hall.'

She looked at him and then smiled. 'I should prefer to have your permission to celebrate with you. I am not suggesting anything elaborate, but some evergreens, candles and pretty ribbons in your drawing room would be most enjoyable.'

'Do as you please. I'm quite sure you will do so with or without my permission.' The rattle of crockery heralded the arrival of his much-needed breakfast. She stood up and was about to go when she turned back and smiled at him. He found himself returning the smile despite his curmudgeonly nature.

'I must tell you, sir, a most amusing thing. When I first read the name above your gate I thought it read, *Devil's Gate*, not Duval's Gate.'

All desire to smile evaporated like snow on a summer's day. 'This house is called Devil's Gate by everyone who knows it. I am descended from a long line of devils. Believe me, if I could send you on your way then I would do so. If anybody was to discover you had stayed with me, not only would your name be blackened, even your fortune would not make you acceptable as a wife to the most avaricious of fortune hunters.'

She nodded but made no comment. His appetite had deserted him and he pushed the tray away. This was a damnable business. He wished with all his heart the girl had stayed at the posting inn and not ventured further and ended up with him.

★　★　★

Her accommodation was in the master suite on the first floor. It had obviously been got ready in a hurry as there was still dust on several of the surfaces and the bed was decidedly damp. This was why she had remained out of it and spent the night in a chair beside the patient.

Sally was doing her best to dry out the mattress but she rather thought it was a lost cause. 'I think I shall move to somewhere smaller. It should be easier to remove the moisture when the bed is not as vast as this one.'

'From what I gather his lordship hasn't been up here for years, from the look of the place nobody has bothered to keep it clean.'

'I don't think he keeps more than a few staff here, I've not seen any maids, have you?'

'I haven't. Therefore, I think we must take over the running of the place whilst we're here. It's so clammy and cold up here even with a fire lit, I wonder if there is somewhere downstairs you could use, miss?'

'An excellent notion, we shall go in search of different accommodation immediately. The major has sent a sleigh to collect our belongings. They should be here later today and we need somewhere to put them.'

Downstairs wasn't particularly clean but at least it was warmer. The drawing room, an elegant chamber that ran half the length of the house, was quite acceptable even to someone with such high standards as herself. The furniture was a tad old-fashioned, but nonetheless polished to a high shine and the upholstery was clean. The curtains, which hung in festoons around each window, had obviously not been drawn for years.

'I don't think we should touch those as they would probably disintegrate. It's fortunate there are shutters to keep out the draughts.' Honour opened the double doors that divided this chamber from the other end to discover a music room. 'There is a pianoforte, a harp and a selection of stringed instruments.'

Sally pointed to a further pair of double doors in the centre of the wall that faced the windows. 'Shall we see where those lead, miss?'

When they were opened they saw another reception room, this one less spacious than the other, but equally well appointed. The view from the windows was exceptional as it looked over an expanse of grass populated with deer and then drew the eye on to the lake.

'I think I shall use this for myself. We shall be staying here for the next few weeks so we might as well make ourselves comfortable.'

There was no door on the far side of this small drawing room, the exit was opposite the windows and led into a spacious passageway with walls lined with portraits of long gone ancestors.

'Before we explore further I need to think exactly where his lordship's apartment is situated. I have no desire to barge in there without invitation.' She stood with her eyes closed attempting to visualise the route she had taken from his bedchamber to the central staircase and entrance hall.

'This building is a large rectangular shape as far as I can work out. We are standing in the centre section, the major's rooms run parallel to the grand drawing room but on the other side of the establishment. Therefore, it should be safe enough to look inside these rooms here.'

'I'll knock, shall I, just in case?' Sally asked.

She nodded and her maid banged on the door with unnecessary force. There was no sound of angry footsteps approaching, in fact, complete silence. They could investigate in here.

'My word! This would be absolutely perfect. This could be my bedchamber and the smaller room through that door could be yours and also be used as my dressing room. How fortunate there is little furniture in either place. That will make it so much easier for the men to get it ready for us.'

She was a guest in this house, and

not a welcome one from what her host had said. If she wanted to claim these for her own she had better do so before he was up, which would probably be tomorrow, if not sooner.

When she made her way to the kitchen she found the six men that were employed inside sitting around the table. They jumped to their feet from her entry. 'I apologise for interrupting you in your own domain, but I have an urgent task and I require all your assistance to complete it as soon as possible.'

There was no grumbling, no argument, in fact all of them seemed happy to help her and even to approve of her high-handed behaviour. After two hours things were arranged to her satisfaction.

'I thank you all for your assistance. I shall be more comfortable down here than upstairs in the damp and cold. Which of you is in charge of the kitchen?'

The young man who stepped forward was the last one she would have picked as a cook. 'I am, miss, for my sins. I ain't no good at it, but no one else would do it.'

'What I need to ask is, are there sufficient provisions in store? I doubt we can send for anything fresh for a week or two at least.'

He beamed and nodded. 'Plenty of food in the larder and the vegetable cellar. Pity is, it won't taste no good by the time I've finished with it.'

This was a problem easily solved. 'Sally and I will run the household. I shall act as temporary mistress.'

Not only the erstwhile cook, but also the other five grinned and slapped each other on the back.

'That'll be capital, miss, we've been muddling along these past months but could do with a woman's hand at the tiller.' The oldest and smartest of the group half-bowed.

'I need to know all your names, I cannot get this house organised in time for the festive period if we do not work closely together.'

Once they had all identified themselves she reassigned them to what would be their new positions in the household. There was only one thing that could prevent her from enjoying herself, and taking charge of a household once again, and that was the master of the house. She had a nasty feeling he might not take kindly to her meddling in his life. He didn't seem like a gentleman who enjoyed being dictated to. If her scheme was to have any chance of success it had to be functioning smoothly by the time he was aware it had happened.

'Sally, you must remain here and prepare a delicious repast for the major's luncheon and an even better dinner. Can I leave this in your capable hands whilst I oversee the arrangement of our luggage?'

The trunks arrived at the same time as a tray with a fluffy omelette, buttered potatoes, and carrots cooked in an orange sauce. There was also a delicious slice of apple pie served with thick cream and a jug of her favourite beverage — coffee.

There must be a hothouse somewhere that she hadn't seen. If his lordship was short of money how on earth could he afford to keep that heated? This establishment was a conundrum, as was its owner, and she intended to solve both puzzles before she left.

★ ★ ★

Ralph had recovered his temper and his appetite long before the welcome sound of someone approaching with his luncheon. It didn't matter how bad the food was, he would eat it anyway. He would not regain his strength if he didn't eat.

Gifford was having difficulty hiding his smile — his valet rarely looked happy. What had changed this morning? Then the tray was placed across his lap and he understood.

'Young Billy had no hand in this. Am

I to assume that Miss Fitzroy is responsible for preparing this delicious repast?'

'No, my lord, it was Sally her maid. You'll be eating like a king in future.'

He savoured every mouthful and could have eaten twice as much. It made sense for the girl to take over the kitchen if she was so proficient, but he wasn't pleased he had not been consulted.

He finished the jug of coffee and then reluctantly drank the second one of warm, spiced, watered wine. He abhorred alcohol. He had vivid memories of the drunken debauchery that had taken place under this roof whilst he hid in the schoolroom hoping he would remain unnoticed. He must have been the only boy at his dreadful school that preferred to be there rather than at home.

Both his father and his older brother had perished from the pox. No more than they deserved. He had already abandoned his home when this occurred and used the money his grandmama had left him to purchase himself a set of colours.

When he had been a lowly subaltern he had not been the possessor of the family title, he had never used it in his military life although he had inherited it several years ago.

He had only returned in order to recuperate and had been given strict instructions not to report to Horse Guards until he had been signed off as one hundred percent fit for active duty. Wellington's army would not fight any major battles until spring — plenty of time for him to recover by then. The fact that his scar had torn open wouldn't deter him.

He detested this place and was tempted to put a match to it when he left next time.

★　★　★

He slept soundly for the entire afternoon. He remained in bed as he had been instructed, apart from the time Gifford helped him to the commode. His valet was proving elusive. There was something going on that was being kept from him and he didn't think it was just the fact that he now had a new cook.

He took a deep breath and used his parade ground voice to summon his valet as he had been ignoring the bell. His mouth curved when he heard several things fall loudly to the floor. Gifford rushed in, his face pale, and stood to attention waiting to be interrogated.

It didn't take long to learn the whole truth. Ralph wasn't sure if he was amused or enraged by the presumption of this unknown young lady. He thought about it for a few minutes before putting Gifford out of his misery.

'It is a *fait accompli*. I should have been consulted but I can see why I was not. I would probably have refused permission without considering the benefits of this new arrangement. It was none of your doing, so you can relax. I shall discuss the matter in depth with the person concerned when I am up tomorrow. I recall she said something about Desdemona having nine healthy puppies. How did she know?'

This time he was astounded at what he was told. He waved his man away and settled back against the comfortable pillows. He reviewed the information he had gleaned about his uninvited guest, and the more he considered it, the more he realised that he was the lucky one, not she. He would give her a beargarden jaw, she would expect that much, but afterwards he would thank her for her intervention with his bitch and for taking over the running of his household. To have palatable meals even for so short a time was something to celebrate.

3

After unpacking the trunks Honour went to see how Sally was managing. She could hear the men drinking tea in the servants' hall, taking a well-earned break, as she passed by.

The kitchen was massive, could cater for hundreds rather than a handful. Her erstwhile dresser was dismembering chickens on the central scrubbed, wooden table.

'Are they for dinner? I enjoyed my luncheon, was it well-received elsewhere?'

'His lordship sent back empty plates. He'll not kick up a fuss about the changes as long as he gets good food. Did you want anything, miss? I've got a tray of scones baking which will be ready very soon.'

'Nothing to eat, thank you. This room is remarkably well equipped, if a little grimy.'

'I reckon there used to be big parties here in the past. We'll not go hungry; the larders are well-stocked and I found shelves of preserves, chutneys, pickles, conserves to last until the summer.'

'Good heavens, that's no concern of ours. We shall be leaving here as soon as I reach my majority and am safe from my cousin.'

'Do you have everything arranged in your apartment, miss? I can't be in two places at once, you know.'

'I am well aware of that, Sally, and can manage perfectly well without a dresser whilst I am residing here. Obviously, I have no wish to dine in solitary splendour. I should like another tray sent to me in my new abode.'

'It'll be ready at five o'clock. These birds should make a tasty stew even though they're a bit long in the tooth. There are ten men who live in, four who work outside and six that work in, as well as the two of us and his lordship. I can't get it done before then if I'm to feed everyone.' She gestured with her head towards

43

the chamber in which the men were drinking tea. 'I gave them permission to take a rest for a quarter of an hour. The two lads that you assigned to the kitchen will be back to assist me shortly.'

'The house needs a thorough clean before I can even think about preparing it for the festive period.'

Sally grinned. 'What does the master think to that? It's all very well cleaning and cooking, but decorating the house in the old-fashioned way?'

'He has given his permission as long as he is not involved. I shall leave you to your culinary duties and get on with mine. If the weather clears a little I shall send someone to the nearest village and see if we can employ some temporary female staff.'

This room was now pleasantly warm, the shutters had been closed and the silver candelabra on the mantelshelf cast a flickering golden light around the place. She took one of the candles and quickly ignited the three other candlesticks. She wanted to be able to see clearly the faces of the men she was going to speak to.

After her mama had died from the sweating sickness it had just been Papa and her. She had been still in the schoolroom, barely a woman grown, but she had abandoned her childish dreams of having a London Season and taken over the tasks as chatelaine of the vast estate.

His title had passed to her cousin, but the estates were not entailed and he had left everything, including his fleet of trading ships, to her. They had travelled together, she had seen places few other young ladies would ever go, and believed herself more than competent to continue his thriving business. Unfortunately, as a mere female, she was not expected to own property in her own name or make decisions for herself.

If she was a widow, however, she would be free to do as she pleased. It had always been in the back of her mind to find herself an ancient husband, one who was too feeble to interfere with her life. Then as soon as he went to meet his maker she would be able to run her life and her business herself. Of course, she would be the best possible wife she could for the few short years, possibly months, that this mythical husband would be alive. That would be a small price to pay in order to have control of her affairs.

She had pulled the bell-strap and waited to see if this summons was answered promptly. There was a polite tap on the half-open door a considerable time later, and Cooper, the new butler, stepped in.

'I apologise if I have kept you waiting, miss, but it were a hard job working out which room you were ringing from. The master never bothers with such things, he just opens the door and yells.'

'That information does not surprise me. There are things I require to know about the neighbourhood. I would like to take on some female staff, find a personal maid for the next few weeks I shall be here, as well as some girls to do the laundry and so on.'

He shook his head. 'You'll not find anyone willing to work here, not anyone local that is.' He shifted uncomfortably from foot to foot but didn't elaborate.

'Lord Duval told me about his unpleasant parent and brother. Surely, if they know that there is a respectable young woman residing here . . . ' Her cheeks flamed; she realised the stupidity of what she had said. No respectable young woman would be living in a bachelor household and especially one so notorious as this.

She recovered her composure and continued. 'Perhaps it would be better not to mention I am here in the circumstances. However, this does not change the fact that we need more staff if we are all to be comfortable. I know I shall not be here for many weeks, but whilst I am I would like things to be as they should.

'Perhaps if you went further afield, and offered a substantial wage as well as good accommodation and excellent food, you would be able to find half a dozen girls willing to come, despite the appalling reputation of this house.'

'I reckon you're right, miss, but there ain't any spare blunt to pay them.'

'I shall take care of that. Forgive me for asking such a delicate question, but I am intrigued to know how you came to be working for his lordship if this house was unoccupied until he returned to recuperate?'

'Gifford has always been with him, he's his orderly. It were he that found us.'

'I see. Another thing I should like to know before you go, how can there be a functioning hothouse if the place had been left empty for years?'

'Only the house were empty, the master kept up the grounds, the gardens and made sure none of his tenants suffered. He never kept a penny of his prize money for himself, but sent it back here. He has a loyal and efficient factor taking care of things.'

'If that is the case, then I cannot see a difficulty in recruiting local girls. Whatever this place was in the past, now things are quite different. How long has his lordship been a soldier?'

'Since he was a lad, this'll be the first time he's lived here in more than fifteen years.'

'How long is it since he inherited the title?'

'That would be five, no six, years ago.'

'Excellent news. He has been a good landlord, has proved himself to be a gentleman. If the sledge was able to go to my carriage and return with my trunks then it can go tomorrow and find me the maids that I require.'

Cooper frowned. It was not his place to disagree with his betters. 'You will do as I bid if you value your position, do I make myself quite clear?'

'Yes, miss, I'll send Fred. He has family nearby.'

She turned her back making it clear he was dismissed and heard the door close quietly behind him. Good heavens! How long did Duval think it took to show that he wasn't a rakehell like his father and brother had been?

* * *

Ralph was prowling around his bedchamber. Regardless of what he'd been told by the officious young lady who had taken over his household, he was resolved to see what she had done.

He was perfectly capable of dressing himself but for some peculiar reason his closet was empty. He did not have an extensive wardrobe, but the only items still folded neatly on the shelves were his uniforms and his evening rig — neither of which would be suitable for daywear. Then he recalled that the girl had said something of the sort — he had thought her to be jesting.

He suspected the chit had colluded with his orderly to have them removed so he couldn't get dressed, and he didn't intend to disturb Gifford until the usual time. He was drawn to the window at first light by the sound of the runners of the sledge crunching over the snow.

Without a second thought he flung back the shutters, pushed open the window and roared at the unfortunate driver. To his amazement whoever was holding the reins ignored his command to stop. There was no doubt in his mind that he had been heard, whoever it was, muffled in a greatcoat with the collar turned up, had jumped as if stuck with a hatpin. Yet still he had been ignored.

He watched in frustration as the sleigh vanished from sight around the bend in the drive. Where the hell was he going? This was his domain. He would not be treated as if he was a simpleton unable to make decisions for himself.

The fact that he had bare feet, and only his nightshirt beneath his robe, made no difference to him. He stormed from the room and headed for the main part of the house. He pounced on a young man who was on his hands and

51

knees scrubbing the boards. 'Where will I find Miss Fitzroy?' Ralph glared and the pail tipped, spreading sudsy water in a growing puddle around the servant's knees.

'I'll show you, my lord, she ain't upstairs no more, she's turned a couple of rooms into her apartment.' He scrambled to his feet, the sacks tied about his waist dripping onto his trousers. He ran, his boots clattering, through the house and stopped in front of a door. 'In there, sir. That's the sitting room.'

Ralph didn't bother to knock, after all it was his own house, and strode in. Who was the more astonished by his abrupt entrance it would have been hard to say. His quarry was standing by her bed in her nightgown and now he was in her bedchamber in a similar state of undress.

'I was told this was your sitting room.'

She recovered her aplomb and nimbly jumped back into bed and pulled the covers up to her chin so not an inch of her was visible apart from her face. It was a very attractive face. Her golden hair was pulled back in a single thick, lustrous braid which dangled enticingly over her shoulder. Her eyes were a deep blue, almost black, this morning.

'Lord Duval, leave this room immediately. How dare you burst in here and in your nightwear?'

He couldn't prevent his mouth from curling. She was quite adorable when she was outraged. 'As I said, Miss Fitzroy, I was misinformed . . . '

She shot up in the bed. 'Do you think it makes it any better that you mistakenly came into my bedroom instead of my sitting room without permission and without clothes?'

He was unused to being shouted at — it was usually he who did the yelling. He ignored her continued protests and picked up a bentwood chair and carried it to within a yard of her bed. 'Please, Miss Fitzroy, I might be old but I'm not deaf. I can hear you perfectly well without you screaming at me like a fishwife.'

As he was about to sit the impossible happened. She stretched out and picked up a solid, silver candlestick and hurled it with admirable precision at his head. His excellent reflexes allowed him to duck the missile, but it missed him by a whisker. It sailed across the room and crashed into the glass-fronted bureau. Shards of glass and splinters flew in all directions.

She turned in an instant from a screaming banshee trying to kill him into someone concerned for his welfare. 'Don't move, my lord, you have bare feet, they will be lacerated as the carpet around you is smothered with glass.'

'And that applies equally to yourself, young lady. So, we are at an impasse, neither of us can move until your maid appears to remedy the situation.'

'Fiddlesticks to that! The splinters are where you are sitting, the other side of my bed is perfectly safe.' No sooner had she spoken than she tossed back the covers and jumped out of bed. There was a flash of bare ankle and then she vanished into the next room.

He was now marooned in a sea of glass and could see no way out of it unless he risked his feet being injured. There was the sound of something being moved, a clatter and then she reappeared with a small rug draped over her arm.

'This should do the trick.' He caught another glimpse of naked flesh as she scrambled across the bed and he caught his breath. He sat rigid whilst she tossed the rug onto the floor making it safe for him to move.

'I suggest that you make yourself scarce, Miss Fitzroy, I am not comfortable having you here when you have only your nightgown on.'

Her expression changed to one of horror. 'I had quite forgotten. I apologise.' She pulled off the thick comforter and draped it around herself before scampering away.

Wherever the sleigh had gone, there was nothing he could do about it and he might as well return to his own domain and hope that Gifford had arrived with his missing garments.

His fury was mercurial, he was infamous for his quick temper, but whoever was on the receiving end knew he would be forgiven as quickly as he had been found wanting.

His valet met him at the door. 'I was about to go in search of you, my lord. You have bare feet.'

'How observant of you, I might not have noticed if you had not drawn my intention to it. I take it my clothes are back where they should be?'

'They are, sir, and there's hot water for your ablutions.'

This was a welcome change as there was rarely such a thing in the morning. He was shaved, washed and dressed in rapid time. An officer soon learned to tumble from bed and be ready to ride in minutes when he was at war.

The third time that Gifford looked

askance at him he was forced to comment. 'Out with it, man, have I grown horns and a tail overnight? I am becoming irritated by your constant scrutiny.'

'I don't reckon I've ever seen you so, so happy, my lord. I'm not a great believer in the Almighty, any more than you are, but I reckon the arrival of Miss Fitzroy is a blooming miracle.'

'Happy? Hardly that. However, I will admit to feeling less miserable than I usually am. Do you know why the sledge went out so early?'

His man looked shifty. 'No idea, major, probably something was left behind in the coach.'

This was a perfectly rational explanation but for some reason he didn't believe it to be the truth. He had no intention of grilling his orderly, he would demand an explanation from the perpetrator of the expedition as soon as she left the safety of her own apartment.

57

4

Honour had never dressed so quickly in her life. It was unlikely that objectionable gentleman would return to her rooms but she was taking no chances. Sally had kindly laid out her clothes before going down to the kitchens to begin her new, hopefully temporary, life as the cook.

Her gown was a deep burgundy, with high neck, long sleeves and plenty of room for an extra petticoat, which was essential in this inclement weather. She didn't bother to rebraid her hair but merely twisted the plait, that dangled down her back, around her head in a coronet and shoved pins in haphazardly. Her appearance was not important, as long as she was correctly dressed it would have to do.

The fire had gone out, not even a glowing ember in the bottom of the grate for her to put kindling on. She must suppose that the new footmen, unlike a chambermaid, had been reluctant to come into her apartment whilst she was still in bed. The sooner she got some female staff the better.

She had told Sally she would eat in the breakfast room in future and thus save the bother of bringing a tray across the house. It was her intention to be in possession of the chamber before he stormed in demanding answers — she wasn't quite sure what it was he had got a burr under his saddle about, but whatever it was, she wouldn't be cowed. He was twice her size and perfectly within his rights to be angry that she had interfered with his life so drastically.

The good Lord had brought her here for a purpose. She wasn't so arrogant as to believe it was for her sake, although she had to admit, she had rather fallen on her feet. She giggled. She had actually fallen on top of him — but the sentiment still stood.

Today should be interesting and there was nothing she liked more than adventure and excitement. No, she was here to put right the major's life. He thought of himself as a monster, depraved like his father and brother, but he was nothing of the sort. By the time she left she was determined he would understand this for himself.

The shutters were still closed as it was scarcely light. There were welcome sounds coming from the breakfast parlour that indicated the chafing dishes were being put out. She sailed in, confident she was there first and almost tripped over her feet.

'Good morning again, Miss Fitzroy. As you can see I am here before you, as is the food. Would you care to be seated and I will serve you as a gentleman ought?'

'Thank you, my lord, I would prefer to select my own breakfast, but I appreciate your kind offer.' She waited for the explosion but he merely nodded and continued to heap his plate with something from every dish.

She did the same but took considerably less. On the table were two large silver jugs — one contained chocolate, the other coffee. Again, she was perplexed that a masculine household would have something so feminine as chocolate available.

He didn't offer to pour her either beverage. She put down her food and then reached across for the coffee pot just as he did the same. The result was inevitable. They both retracted their hands so violently the jug started to tumble sideways. His lightning reactions caught it and he righted it without spilling a drop.

'Bravo, that was well done, Major. Now that you have hold of the jug would you be kind enough to pour me some?'

His expression was hard to read but he did as she asked. He then tipped some into his own delicate porcelain cup and resumed his seat. He ignored her and tucked into his meal as if he'd been denied provisions for days rather than hours.

She watched him with amusement for a few moments and then picked up her own cutlery. Everything on her plate was perfectly cooked and quite delicious. Sally was probably a better cook than she was a maid, but rarely had the opportunity to show her skills.

They ate in silence and finished at the same time. 'More coffee, Miss Fitzroy?'

'That would be delightful, thank you, my lord.'

He looked up and his eyes reflected his amusement. 'Delightful? That's doing it too brown, my dear.'

She couldn't hold his gaze and looked down and fiddled with her napkin to hide her nervousness. She much preferred him when he was roaring at her, she could deal with that, his charm was far more dangerous.

'Why did you come bursting into my bedchamber like a lunatic?' This wasn't what she had intended to say but, as always, she spoke without thinking.

The jug jerked and coffee slopped onto the white cloth making an unpleasant brown stain. He completed the task and then pushed the cup towards her. He then drained his own and refilled it. She watched the strong column of his neck as he swallowed and a wave of heat settled in a most unexpected place.

He looked up and pinned her with an arctic gaze. 'I think perhaps, Miss Fitzroy, you might need to rephrase your question.' His tone was even but his message clear.

'I beg your pardon for calling you a lunatic. But I cannot think that a man in his right senses would do something so . . . so unpardonable.' This was hardly a conciliatory response but it was the best she could do.

'I am not sure if I am about to turn you over my knee or applaud you. You are certainly a most unusual young lady.'

This threat did not frighten her as

somehow she knew he would never raise his hand to her or any other woman. Therefore, she became reckless. 'I think that one might say that a pot is calling the kettle black, sir.'

'Indeed? Are you not bothered that I might make good my threat?'

'No, I trust you. You might be quick-tempered, but you are not a violent man — or certainly not where anyone weaker than yourself is concerned.'

His smile made her stomach lurch. 'That is the prettiest compliment anyone has ever paid me and I thank you for it. You have not known me for more than a day and yet you trust me not to harm you.'

'As we are now on more amicable terms, can I enquire as to why you did come to my rooms this morning?'

'I want to know why the sledge went out at dawn. As far as I know we are not in need of anything or . . . '

'On that point you are incorrect, I need more staff inside if I am to be comfortable for these next few weeks. I sent someone to find some. Do not poker up at me, sir, I shall be paying their wages.'

Suddenly the atmosphere changed. He surged to his feet and slammed his hands down on the table making the crockery and cutlery jump. She almost left her chair in shock.

'This is my house. God's teeth, woman! How dare you make such decisions as if you are chatelaine here?'

She flattened herself against the chair back unable to catch her breath and respond for a few seconds. Then she recovered her equilibrium, cleared her throat and attempted to sound as if she wasn't almost incapable of speech. 'You did give me permission to run this house for you whilst I am here.' His expression softened somewhat and all might have been well if she had left it there, but this was not her way, she had to speak what was in her mind.

'I expect you were not quite yourself when you did so, having lost so much blood. Indeed, you should not really be up, but resting in your bed for at least another day.' She smiled brightly, but it was an effort. 'I am sorry if you are displeased with the arrangements I have made, but I fear it is too late to undo the changes.'

He subsided into his chair and her hands unclenched. She waited for him to speak, for until he did so she had no notion if he was indeed recovered from his fury or just biding his time.

'It is I who must apologise to you, Miss Fitzroy. I can be a little abrupt sometimes.'

She raised an eyebrow and he laughed out loud. 'All right, I have a shockingly bad temper. I expect I shall be roaring and shouting at you half a dozen times a day so you had better get used to it.'

It was her turn to laugh. 'I shall endeavour not to infuriate you. However, I cannot promise I shall be able to do so as you are so very easy to displease.'

He sat back and folded his arms across his impressive chest. 'I might have been a trifle out of sorts, but my memory is not defective, young lady. I recall exactly what I gave you permission to do and it was not to turn my household upside down and appoint staff. I said that you could decorate the drawing room if you so wished.'

Her cheeks coloured beneath his scrutiny as he was perfectly correct. 'I hardly think it matters now that it is done. I have been running a household far bigger than this for the past four years so you may have no worries on that score. I can assure you once you have become accustomed to the new regime you will be glad that I have done it for you.'

* * *

Ralph was rarely lost for words but on this occasion he was. The girl was impossible. She refused to be browbeaten into submission, refused to accept that she was in the wrong, and blithely continued to do as she pleased regardless of his wishes.

'I am not disputing the fact that you are competent, but . . . ' He shrugged theatrically. 'I surrender, I have been routed by a superior force. Go ahead, Miss Fitzroy, and do your worst. I warn you that I shall not be so easily vanquished next time.'

She rose gracefully to her feet and curtsied as if she was in the presence of royalty. 'Yes, my lord, your comments have been noted.' She spun and her skirts whirled around her giving him a satisfactory glimpse of her delectable ankles. Then she was gone and the room seemed empty without her.

He was still hungry, not something that happened often. He refilled his plate and was halfway through it when he heard the unmistakable crunch of the sledge returning. He dropped his cutlery and strode to the window.

What he saw made him clutch the window frame for support. There were half a dozen girls huddled in the back under furs and rugs clutching their meagre belongings on their laps. How could this be? No sensible mother would allow her daughter to go into service in this den of iniquity.

How had this been accomplished? He left the remains of his breakfast and went in search of answers. Cooper was talking to the girl but saw him approaching and vanished as if by magic leaving the interfering baggage alone. 'Girls, Miss Fitzroy? How did you accomplish that?'

'Shall we go into the drawing room where we can be comfortable, it is decidedly draughty in the hall?' Instead of turning into the double doors ahead she walked briskly down the passageway to a smaller room that had once, many years ago, been his mother's favourite.

There was a huge fire burning in the grate, the room was warm, far more welcoming than the vast drawing room he had expected her to use. This was another change to his routine, but a sensible one so he decided to let it pass without comment.

She took a seat on the sofa on the right of the fire and he sat on the one opposite. 'Well, I am waiting for your answer.'

When she had finished explaining he was for the second time that morning silenced. He closed his eyes in order to consider what he had just learnt. Could it be possible that he was no longer considered a danger to society? That the sins of the fathers, grandfathers and brothers were not to be heaped upon his head?

It was as if a weight he hadn't realised he was carrying slithered from his shoulders. 'This is a revelation to me, my dear, I have never ventured into the villages in my demesne, I was too ashamed. I owe you a debt of gratitude that I shall find hard to repay.'

Her smile was like a blow to the chest. He had thought her pretty enough, but he had been wrong. She was quite beautiful both inside and out. Infuriating, interfering, and opinion- ated, but without doubt quite the most perfect specimen of womanhood he had ever encountered.

He stared at her, seeing her with fresh eyes and she must have seen something to alarm her as she suddenly jumped to her feet and rushed to the door. 'I must go, my lord, I need to speak to the girls who have just arrived and give them their new duties.'

He stretched out his legs towards the warmth of the fire, put his hands behind his head, yawned and promptly fell asleep. He was woken by the sound of someone adding logs and coal to the fire. Lazily he opened one eye.

'Beggin' your pardon, my lord, for waking you but the mistress said I must make up the fire regardless.' The speaker was a girl of no more than fifteen or sixteen years of age. She looked at him without fear, with respect, but no more than that.

'Carry on with your duties, I intend

to remain here.' This time he lifted his legs onto the sofa so he was more comfortable. He was forced to admit that both Miss Fitzroy — no, in future she would be . . . ? He slammed his boots back on the floor making the unfortunate maid drop the log she was about to put into the flames.

He grinned and strode from the room. He could not go another minute without knowing the first name of the girl who had inexplicably broken through his reserve and touched his heart. Eventually he tracked her down in what must once have been the housekeeper's domain. She was perusing a ledger, nodding and smiling at what she saw.

'I need to know your given name — mine is Ralph — I'm not sure if I have already told you that.'

She squeaked and dropped the book with a thump on the boards. 'I had no idea you were there. You must not creep up on a person like that. For a big man you move remarkably quietly.'

He snatched a chair, spun it round and straddled it. After folding his arms along the top, he returned to the attack. 'What is your name?'

'It is Honour. And you did tell me that your name was Ralph. Are you suggesting we should abandon formality so soon in our acquaintance and address each other as Ralph and Honour?'

'One thing I can say about you without fear of contradiction, sweetheart, is that you are not short of wit. I will not hear another, my lord, major or sir — is that clear?'

'Perfectly. I have no desire to stand on ceremony either.' She fluttered her eyelashes and then peeked at him in a coy way that made him want to reach out and kiss her breathless. 'After all, if a young lady has seen a gentleman's bare feet she can hardly continue to address him formally.'

He rested his chin on his hands and smiled at her in a way he had never smiled at any other woman. It had the desired effect and her cheeks turned a becoming shade of pink. 'And I, sweetheart, saw part of your delectable anatomy that only a husband should see.'

Her eyes widened and her hands clenched on the book. He watched her struggling with her fury, not sure what she was going to do next. He was prepared to duck if the ledger came towards his head.

'I am disappointed in you, sir. A *gentleman* would not have referred to such a thing.' Her lips curved but the smile did not reach her eyes. 'Was there anything else you wanted to speak about? As you can see, I am extremely busy.'

Ralph almost fell off his chair. How had this girl the temerity to dismiss him as if he were of no account? He had two options — he could leave the room in high dudgeon or remain and continue to annoy her. He decided on the latter. 'I am going nowhere, sweetheart, it might have escaped your notice but this is my house, not yours, and I can do as I damn well please.'

'In which case, it is I that shall leave. In future I shall lock my apartment doors as you obviously have no respect for my privacy.'

The ledger slammed shut making her feelings plain. She stood up, nodded frostily, and sailed past him with her nose in the air. He was tempted to put out his hand and restrain her but thought better of it. He leaned forward and picked up the book she had been staring at so avidly and flicked open the pages.

It was the list of purchases for the household since his return. It also listed the names of the staff and the amount they had been paid in wages. He had no idea who had been keeping the accounts, but they had done an excellent job. Also recorded were the sales of the first litters of puppies and that made satisfactory reading. Why anyone should pay so much for a hound he had no idea. He had been given a breeding pair by a grateful family he had saved from a French corsair. Gifford had acquired two more bitches and the recent litter was the fourth since he had got back.

He was about to close the book again when today's entry caught his eye. This was written in different handwriting — it must have been what she was doing when he interrupted her. There were the names of the six maids she had employed, which was only to be expected in a well-run household. What held his attention was the vast sum of money that had been added to the money received column.

A wave of fury engulfed him and if she had been within arm's reach he might well have strangled her, so angry was he. Then instead of crashing back the chair and going in search of her, the anger ebbed and he found himself laughing quietly.

He was now a kept man. He closed the book, returned the chair and strolled from the room. A kept woman would normally be referred to as the mistress of the gentleman concerned — did that make him the master? He was still smiling as he walked past the two footmen who exchanged bewildered glances at the sight.

The house seemed different somehow, more welcoming, less threatening and for the first time since he had been a small boy he didn't look about the place with dislike. He stopped in the centre of the hall and looked up at the magnificent chandelier, the intricate moulding on the ceiling, the carved oak staircase with its festoons of grapes, cherubs and birds. He had always hated Devil's Gate, but in the space of two short days Honour had begun to turn it into a house he could perhaps be content to live in.

The puppies were doing well thanks to her, and now his men and dependents were secure in his employment. He owed her a lot. There was one thing he could do that might slightly redress the balance.

He raised his voice and yelled for someone to attend him. Three of the outdoor men were at his side in minutes. 'I want Miss Fitzroy's carriage brought here. I believe the rear axle is broken so it will be necessary to take a diligence of some sort and load it onto that.'

Fred, he recognised him now as the driver of the sledge that morning, touched his cap. 'There ain't anything big enough here, my lord, but I reckon Farmer Jones has something that would do.'

'Can I leave it to you to organise this?'

'You can, sir. There's not much doing on the fields with the weather as it is, I can round up a dozen or two men from the village who will be only too willing to help.'

Yesterday he would have been astounded by this news, but now he understood that his determination to be different from previous holders of the title had paid dividends. He had not visited any of the farms, cottages or villages that he was responsible for, he had left that to his estate manager. When he had been transported from the battlefront no one had expected him to survive. Against all the odds he had slowly recovered although it had taken him the best part of six months to do so.

Since then he had not ridden anywhere apart from his park, not ventured out to see how things were in the neighbourhood as he had no expectation of being received favourably. As soon as the weather cleared he would remedy that, and visit all the farms, hamlets and the villages that he had been supporting with his prize money.

He left Fred, obviously a capable young man, to arrange for the retrieval of the carriage and its repair and was about to return to the house when he saw a small sleigh, pulled by a single horse, approaching at speed. His eyesight was excellent and he recognised the driver as Ensley, his factor. What was bringing this man from the warmth of his comfortable house on such a day?

5

Honour regretted her outburst, after all she was supposedly a guest and yet she had taken control of the household as if she was a member of his family. Perhaps she would leave it until later before apologising, yet again. They seemed to do nothing but argue and apologise — but it was certainly invigorating.

The house was humming with activity, everywhere she looked there were busy servants with smiling faces and she was certain that in a very short space of time it would be exactly how she wanted it. There was nothing she liked better than organising things and she had been sadly idle since her dear father had departed this world.

Papa had died last year whilst they were travelling in India. He had suffered from a fatal apoplexy, one moment he had been laughing and talking the next he was dead. They had both known that his time on this earth was limited, his physician had warned him he had a weak heart, so they have been determined to pack in as much living as they could before he left her.

It had taken her a further six months to return to England, contact the lawyers, and then reluctantly travel to her cousin as he was now her legal guardian until she came of age. She shuddered as she thought about the few weeks she had spent under his roof. The man was a gambler and determined to force her into a marriage with her second cousin. Robert was also unpleasant, but unlike his parent, he was a weak man and would do as he was told.

They had left her no alternative but to flee, as the closer it got to her name day the more concerned she was about her safety. Sally had pointed out to her that Cousin Robert would inherit her money if she should die before she reached her majority. Papa had arranged matters so that after that date she could control her own destiny, as much as any woman could.

She had had no particular destination in mind, had just wanted to put as much distance between herself and her cousins as she could. It had been fortuitous that the carriage had come to grief and she had found Duval's Gate. Ralph, for he was that in her thoughts now, would keep her safe from her deadly relatives. She feared that she had walked into a different kind of danger coming here, as her host was an extremely attractive gentleman — far too charming as far as she was concerned.

Sally was preparing a more elaborate dinner tonight, but they would still not use the enormous dining room, they would eat in the breakfast parlour. She rang the bell and Cooper appeared.

'I would like to see the orangery, exactly where is it situated?'

'It's attached to the stable block, I don't reckon you want to go out there today, miss, far too cold. The heat from the horse muck keeps it nice and warm. His lordship kept it, and the kitchen garden, the park and so on, in good order even though he ignored the house.'

'Thank you for the information. I shall not venture out there today. Another matter entirely — I would like greenery, holly, ivy, mistletoe — that sort of thing — to be gathered and put in the flower room. I intend to decorate the small drawing room, the grand hall and the breakfast room for the festive period. I should also like the fireplace in the grand hall to be cleared and a yule log brought in that we can light on Christmas Eve.'

'I don't reckon the master will take too kindly to all that, miss . . . '

She drew herself up to her full height and stared at him. 'You forget your place, Cooper, and if you intend to retain it you will not do so again. Do as you are bid and do it now.'

He flushed painfully, muttered something unintelligible and then stomped off. If he was to remain as senior male servant he would have to improve his manners. She was not one to stand on ceremony, but she would not be gainsaid by a servant.

She retreated to the small drawing room not wishing to promote any further insolence and have to reprimand him a second time. If she were being honest with herself, she understood that he was just being a loyal servant to his master, after all she had only arrived two days ago and was already ordering everyone around.

She picked up the book she had discarded earlier but it couldn't hold her attention. What was it about this place, this gentleman, that had so stirred her feelings that she felt as if she belonged here? She would have to be wary if she did not desire to put herself in an invidious position and be obliged to remain here because she had been compromised.

Ralph had remained in the little office after she had departed. She wondered what his reaction had been when he saw how much money she was going to contribute to his finances. Although she could not yet access the principle of her trust fund, the interest from that was more than most families had to live on for a year. The money would be transferred to the household account as soon as she could send a letter to her bankers.

After an hour she tossed the book aside and stood up, restless, not sure how to occupy her time when her head was filled with images of a raven-haired gentleman. She was about to ring for some refreshment when she was startled by the sound of heavy footsteps. The door flew open and Ralph came in, his expression was grim.

★   ★   ★

Honour waited calmly to hear what he had to say.

'You were obliged to abandon your carriage the day before yesterday. My estate manager went that way this morning and it was gone. There was evidence that several horses and a large cart had been there. I'm at a loss to know how such a thing could have happened so quickly.'

'Then I can enlighten you, it will be my cousin, Sir Edward Fitzroy, who has taken it. Ralph, I must leave here at once. Do you have a carriage I can use?'

He had feared it was something of the sort. She looked calm but when he touched her arm she was shaking. 'Sit, sweetheart, you must tell me everything about this man so I can be prepared for his arrival.'

'I told you, I must leave before he comes. I have brought more than enough trouble to your household without adding anymore.'

He guided her gently to the *chaise longue* and obediently she sat. He took her hands and hoped by holding them he would give her the reassurance she needed, that he could convince her he was more than capable of taking care of her.

'I might be recovering from a serious injury, my dear, but I am a soldier to my backbone. I have more than a dozen loyal men at my disposal and sufficient weaponry in my gunroom to equip them. Is your cousin likely to bring more?' He had thought she would smile at his hyperbole, tell him that he was overreacting, but instead she nodded.

'He is a desperate man, I fear he will go to any lengths to snatch me back before my name day. If I were to die then everything would go to him. He has more than a dozen retainers loyal to him, and he could well hire more. People could be killed, and I will not have that on my conscience.'

'God's teeth! It will not come to that. As you noticed on your arrival I have locked gates and a six-foot wall along the entire boundary that is accessible from the road.'

'But I am certain there are ways to get in that you cannot prevent. He could set fire to the house and then we would all perish.'

'Come now, sweetheart, you are exaggerating the case. Your cousin is a desperate man perhaps, but not a mad one.'

'I think he could well be insane, his behaviour this past few months has been erratic and violent, not just towards me but towards his son and servants.' She snatched her hands back and leapt to her feet. 'I am not going to take that chance, Ralph, I shall leave immediately.'

He towered over her, he was twice her size, but he would never hurt her in any way — and he would die before he let anyone else do so. 'You will do no such thing. You must trust me to do my job. If you will not give me your word that you will remain inside then I shall be forced to have you locked into your apartment.'

She subsided like a deflated pig's bladder. 'I suppose that I must trust you, you are a military man, if you cannot protect me then I might as well hand myself over and save all the aggravation.'

'Do I have your word?' He knew her

well enough, even after so short an acquaintance, to realise she was prevaricating, avoiding having to promise to remain.

'Very well, I promise I shall not try to leave.'

He smiled, then she continued. 'But I shall only do so if you do not shut me out. I want to be kept fully informed of everything that is happening and not fobbed off with platitudes.'

'I shall tell you when I have everything in place. They have a day's advantage and I cannot sit here bandying words with you any longer if I am to . . . '

'Then go, it is you that is bandying not me.'

He was on his feet immediately. 'Please, sweetheart, remain inside until this business is over. You must forget about visiting the orangery, the puppies or anywhere else that involves leaving the house.'

'I am not a widgeon, sir, I have plenty to occupy me for the moment.' She smiled and something changed for him. Then the colour left her cheeks and she was once more on her feet, her face anguished.

'I sent some of your outside men into the wood to collect greenery. Have they returned? I shall never forgive myself if anything untoward has occurred because of my desire to decorate the house.'

'I'll find out. I'm sure they are perfectly fine. Remain here and I'll send word to you.'

He hoped his words and smile had reassured her, that she hadn't seen the worry in his eyes. He strode through the house making decisions as he went. First, he needed to speak to Gifford. His valet listened without comment.

'Right you are, Major, no need to alarm anyone as yet. I'll nip down and see what's what outside.'

'Do that, it could be that we're worrying unnecessarily — but I have a bad feeling about this. All Fitzroy's men had to do were make enquiries in the village and they would have known something was going on. This is the nearest house to where the carriage broke its axle so Fitzroy must know his quarry is here.'

Gifford vanished through the dressing room door, taking the passageway that bisected the house, the one put in especially for the use of servants so they wouldn't be seen about their business.

He went from room to room checking the windows were latched and then closing the shutters. Then he inspected each door, including the ones used by the staff, and firmly bolted them. Those working here needed to know why there was the need for caution, but he wasn't sure how urgent this matter was, he would wait until Gifford returned before going down to the servants' hall and speaking to those that worked for him.

His valet returned. 'The sledge went out more than an hour ago and hasn't returned. They were going to Home Wood, I reckon it would take them half an hour to get there, an hour to fill the sledge, and another half an hour to return.'

'In which case they should be visible from an upstairs window. There is a clear view to the wood from the rear of the house.'

They pounded up the stairs and shoulder to shoulder entered one of the guest bedchambers. The tracks left from the sledge and the horse were quite clear, but there was no sign of them returning.

'Gifford, bring everybody inside. Make sure the grooms leave the horses with food and water for the next twenty-four hours, also the dogs.' He frowned and considered what else he could do. 'One of the stableboys must bolt the doors from the inside and then exit through the hayloft. Make sure there are no ladders available for an intruder to use.'

His man saluted, and it didn't seem incongruous that they were both wearing civilian clothes.

'Yes, Major, right away, sir.'

Ralph had promised he would keep Honour fully informed of what was going on. She sat unusually silent whilst he told her everything he knew and what he was doing.

'Are you not going in search of them?'

'I cannot do that at the moment, it is what they would expect to happen. My first priority is to make the house safe, ensure that no one else can be abducted — if that is what has happened.' Better to say they were being held hostage than the alternative, which was that they were already dead.

'I shall come with you when you speak to the staff. I am an expert with firearms, I can handle a musket or a pistol as well as most men. I am also proficient with a foil.'

He drew her into his arms, it was an instinctive thing to do, and she didn't object. 'I hope you will not be called upon to demonstrate your prowess.' He held her close for a moment and dropped a light kiss on the top of her head. It fitted perfectly under his chin.

'I have been thinking in your absence, there is one way we can put a stop to this but I cannot see how it can be accomplished in time.' She tilted her face to look at him. 'You could marry me and then if I die everything would already be yours.'

He started to laugh but then saw she was serious in her suggestion. 'I suppose I should not have been surprised that you have proposed to me. I am already your financial dependent, am I not?'

'Fiddlesticks to that! I am injecting a fraction of my annual interest into your household account. It is only fair that I pay my way as I am your uninvited guest.'

What happened next was inevitable. He cupped the back of her head with one hand and drew her closer so every inch was pressing against him. He paused for a moment to see if she would struggle but instead her hands slid up his chest and entangled themselves in the hair at the back of his neck.

He covered her mouth with his own and their fate was sealed. Only the arrival of Gifford, who cleared his throat noisily, prevented things from getting further out of hand.

He kept one arm around her waist and turned to face his orderly. 'You may be the first to congratulate us, we are to be married at the earliest opportunity.'

If he had announced he was to marry the Queen of Sheba, Gifford could not have looked more shocked. He opened and shut his mouth several times before finding his voice.

'Congratulations, my lord, but is now the time to be thinking of matrimony?'

Honour stepped away and laughed. 'It is the perfect time, Gifford. However, you will need to go to London and obtain a special licence at Doctors' Commons. I shall supply you with my details, no doubt you already know those of the major.'

She sat down at the *escritoire* and

calmly began to write. He drew his man to one side so he could speak to him without being overheard.

'I have no intention of holding her to this, so don't look so appalled. I am not husband material, we both know that.' He explained her reasons and his valet nodded.

'Makes sense now you say that. But I ain't leaving you to fetch a licence, not at the moment. Why don't you send Fred, he is a resourceful young man, I reckon he could do it?'

'If everyone is gathered downstairs we shall come down and speak to them.'

There were no smiling faces in the hall. Sally ran across to join her mistress and they moved into a corner to converse quietly. The remaining outside men, boots respectfully removed, stood together, and they all looked worried.

'We are under attack. Sir Edward Fitzroy believes that he can snatch his cousin from me. That will happen over my dead body — or over his. Miss

Fitzroy came here for my protection and she has it. I hope you are prepared to do your part in keeping her safe.'

He spoke as he always did to his troops, in a moderate tone, looking from one to the other as he did so and making direct eye contact. All of them nodded without hesitation.

Cooper stepped forward. 'The four lads who went in search of greenery have been taken. I'd like to come with you to recover them.'

A murmur of approval ran around the room, the other men surged forward to stand at his side and even the two stableboys joined him.

'Mr Ensley left some time ago to find more volunteers from the village. He has been instructed to send someone to raise the militia. The villagers will approach from the other side and distract who-ever has my men. This will give me an opportunity to make an attack. How many of you can use a firearm?'

There were three others apart from Gifford, Cooper and himself that he thought it would be safe to take.

'Miss Fitzroy is in charge of the defence of the house as she is an excellent shot.' He turned to Cooper. 'Is the exit through the cellars still passable?'

'It is, but a mite mucky, my lord, but I reckon we could get through there all right.'

Satisfied he had everything arranged as he intended he sent Gifford with two others to collect the weapons. His own sword was kept in the armoury, if a small locked room could be so designated, and he would wear that. With two primed and loaded pistols, one in each pocket, he should be ready for anything that occurred.

He beckoned his small party away from the others so he could speak directly to them. Once they were out of earshot he told them what he expected to happen and what their role in this would be.

'We cannot approach directly as we would be seen immediately. We shall travel on foot, of course, and approach from the west, they won't expect us to be coming from the same direction as they did. Make sure you are warmly dressed, have stout boots on, and tie your mufflers around your face so that only your eyes are visible.'

A quarter of an hour later they slipped out of the cellar door and he waited until he heard one of the stableboys bolt it firmly behind them. They were unlikely to have been seen emerging from here as it was behind the laundry and dairy block. There were no longer cows kept at Devil's Gate, but if he was to stay here permanently he would bring back a small herd, just enough to take care of the household's needs.

Why the hell was he thinking about cows now? It had been too long since he had been with the army, he was soft, more a civilian than a soldier nowadays. It would be a long walk and he needed to pace himself. If his new sutures ripped he would be in trouble.

6

Honour double-checked that all the shutters and doors were locked on the ground floor and then insisted that everybody went upstairs. 'We need a fire lit in this room, I shall leave that to the girls. The rest of you will keep watch at the windows and let me know immediately if you see any movement.'

She carefully propped the three muskets, and the paraphernalia needed to fire them, against the wall. When she turned to speak to the men that had been left behind she realised someone was missing. 'Where is Fred? Did he go with his lordship after all?'

One of the other young men shook his head. 'No, miss, he went off a while ago on an errand for the master. He said he would be gone a fair while and wouldn't be back until tomorrow or the next day.'

'Thank you for that information, as long as I know he is not missing, I shall not worry about him. Now, do you three know how to fire a musket or would you like me to show you?'

None of them did but they were quick learners and after an hour she was confident they would be able to at least load and fire the weapon even if they couldn't hit a target. One would load whilst the other two fired.

She could probably do more damage herself, but she wanted to keep them occupied. The six girls had split up and returned with several baskets of logs and coal. Soon the chamber was warm enough to consider removing her cloak but she decided against it, just in case she was obliged to go outside for any reason.

'Jed, I should like you to open a window, not too far, just enough so we can hear what is going on outside.'

Sally was taking this in her stride, but then she had travelled all over the world and been involved in all sorts of excitement without upset. 'I'll take these two with me and bring up some refreshments. No need for us to starve whilst we're on sentry-go.'

'Stay away from the windows just in case whoever is out there has managed to creep close without being seen.'

There was too much time to dwell on the situation. She ran over the events of the past few days to see if she would have done anything differently if she had her time over again. She would certainly have been more careful climbing the gate so that she did not fall on top of Ralph. Apart from that, even with the current unfortunate situation, she could see nothing that she could have changed.

One thing did puzzle her — why had her cousin bothered to take away the carriage? With a broken axle it was no use to anyone. The only possible explanation was that he intended to sell it once it was repaired. The vehicle was recently purchased and would no doubt finance some of the men he had hired to find her.

'Miss, miss, did you hear that? I'm certain that I heard the cart returning. The lads are back and we've been worrying unnecessarily.' Jed had been hanging out of the window, contrary to her instructions, and this was why he had been able to hear activity that wasn't on this side of the house.

Her initial delight was tempered by caution. 'Close the window, do it quietly. You could be right, but it could be a trap. Bring the weapons, we will go to the other side of the house and investigate before we do anything precipitous.'

The chamber they went to was icy, frost patterned the inside of the window, and there were damp patches on the plaster. She raced to the window and threw it up, was about to poke her head out when she thought better of it.

Sure enough, approaching along the tradesmen's lane that ran behind the stable block was the diligence, and there were certainly four muffled men accompanying it. Her breath hissed through her teeth. Sir Edward had certainly stolen her carriage, but he obviously hadn't kidnapped the men she had sent to collect greenery.

The cart was piled high, even from that distance she could see the red berries of the holly catching the sunlight. 'We shall watch for a moment longer, it is better to be safe than sorry. The men are very quiet, should they not be talking to each other?'

⋆ ⋆ ⋆

Ralph led from the front as all good officers did. He kept them in the shadow of the hedges even when it meant the snow was over the top of their boots. No one complained. When the going was better he increased the pace, twenty strides at a walk and then twenty strides at the double. Again, they followed his lead without comment.

He had demonstrated the various hand signals he would use to avoid speaking when they were close to their adversaries. They had been travelling for around half an hour when he raised his fist. He sniffed the air like a wolf — yes — he could smell men and horses not far ahead. He gestured to Gifford to crawl forward on his belly and investigate and his man did so.

He loosened his sword in its scabbard and checked his pistols were primed and ready to fire. He heard faint movement behind him and guessed the men were doing the same.

Gifford beckoned them forward. He dropped to his knees and glanced over his shoulder to see everyone else was doing the same. He slithered through the snow but was unaware of the cold seeping through his breeches, his total concentration was on what was to come. He was battle ready even if he wasn't battle hard.

He kept his head an inch above the snow and raised it a little so he could see why he had been summoned. There was no sign of their riders. He remained vigilant, not moving a muscle, until he was certain the horses were not guarded.

'Gifford with me, the rest of you stay here.' Orders given, he set off bent almost double, keeping one hand on the scabbard to ensure the sword didn't trip him up. This was a manoeuvre he had done many times and his actions were instinctive.

The horses shifted uneasily on their approach but none of them whinnied. Such a sound would carry through the silent, snow-covered trees.

He untethered the furthest one and then he and Gifford released the others. Ralph then grasped its bit and led it away slowly, taking a meandering path, whilst still keeping his outline below its withers. If one of the would-be abductors saw the horses moving they should assume they had become loose and would not be unduly bothered.

As he'd expected all the animals followed and as soon as the last one was behind the hedge he stood up. 'Right,' he gestured at the grooms, 'take these horses back to our stables. One of you will have to go in via the loft window — or fetch the stableboy to do so.'

They could lead a horse each and hopefully the others would want to remain with their stablemates. Most animals would prefer to be inside on a day like this and the nearer they got to buildings the more eager they would be to follow.

He waited until they were out of sight and then returned to the task in hand. It would probably take an hour for them to get back as they would have to keep stopping to collect stray animals.

'Without their horses the villains cannot escape. Gifford and I will go in search of them, I want you two to position yourselves out of sight and to fire at will if they return. If you hit someone that will be a bonus. The racket should be enough to panic them.'

It was eerily silent. Wherever his quarry was, it wasn't here, so why had they left their horses? He pointed to the ground. They could follow the trail of footsteps easily. He was concerned they hadn't come across the missing men but he would remain optimistic until the facts proved otherwise.

There was less snow under the canopy of naked branches, which made travelling both easier and quicker. He had been moving fast for about ten minutes when he raised his hand. They were approaching a clearing.

'This must be where the men were cutting greenery for the house. You can see the evidence in the trees. It's too damn quiet. Where the devil are they all? What have they done with the horse and cart?'

'Over there, Major, I think I saw something beneath that holly tree.'

He followed Gifford's pointing finger and sure enough beneath the trailing branches there was definitely some movement and it definitely wasn't of the animal variety. Thank the good Lord, the men were still alive, or at least one of them was.

'We must approach from the rear,

just in case they have someone guarding them.' This conversation had been conducted in whispers.

They slowly backed away and began a circuitous journey through the trees until they were close enough to be able to hear a rhythmic thumping against the ground, as if someone was drumming their feet. He unbuckled his sword and laid it in the snow, then removed his stiletto from his boot top. Gifford did the same.

He had discarded his greatcoat before his first crawl through the snow, but he didn't feel the cold when he was focused on his job. As he wriggled towards the holly he looked for any signs that there were guards — when he was no more than two yards from his objective he was confident whoever had left his men tied up beneath this tree was no longer there.

'Keep silent, keep still, Gifford and I are coming to release you.' His voice was pitched low and quiet but it carried and the thumping stopped. He wasn't

109

going to stand up, better to complete this mission surreptitiously, not take any unnecessary risks of being discovered.

The four men were bound and gagged but otherwise unhurt. Before removing their gags, he put his finger to his lips and they nodded that they understood they should not speak. In a matter of moments, the ropes were cut and the six of them were slithering backwards until they were safely hidden behind a mound of snow-covered brambles.

'How many were there? Did you hear what their intentions were?'

'They were upon us before we knew it, my lord, I reckon there must have been a dozen at least. They said nought, surly blighters, but they knew their business all right,' one of them said.

'They have the cart with the greenery. I suspect they were hoping to approach the house pretending to be yourselves. How long ago were you attacked?'

'It took us an age to fill the cart with what Miss Fitzroy wanted, my lord, and we was just finishing when we was set upon, I reckon it weren't more than half an hour ago.'

'Did any of you see if they were carrying firearms?'

'Rifles, not muskets, and two of them had swords.' This information was given by the youngest of the four, not much more than a boy, but an observant one.

'Thank you, lad, that is invaluable. Arm yourselves with the largest piece of wood you can find — but remain in cover unless matters get desperate. They cannot get into the house, so now I have you four safe, things are less urgent.'

'Beggin' your pardon, Major, but we've sent the two grooms and them blighters' horses straight into the hornet's nest.'

Cold sweat trickled between Ralph's shoulder blades. It had been too long since he had been in command and his mind was befuddled.

'We must run, God willing we will get there before they do.'

★ ★ ★

Honour gestured that the others keep out of sight, not crowd around the window. She remained hidden behind the folded shutter and watched carefully the approach of the cart. Something had attracted her attention behind the hedge that bordered the track. She screwed up her eyes hoping to improve her vision. She had never been able to see distances as clearly as she could the objects close to her.

She beckoned one of the men to approach and pointed towards the place she thought she had seen something move. 'What do you see over there?'

'There's blighters with weapons, miss, that ain't our boys coming back but someone pretending, hoping to trick us.'

Once away from the window she considered her options. 'How many do you think there were?'

'A fair few, about seven or eight at least.'

'In which case we are ill-prepared to do anything other than remain hidden. We should have closed the shutters up here, but too late to repine. We cannot do so now as it would immediately draw attention to the fact that we are on the upper floor.'

'What are we going to do, miss?'

'We shall return to the chamber that is warm and comfortable and remain safe there until we are rescued.'

They trooped back and as they arrived so did the trays of coffee, chocolate, and spiced wine. She thought the latter a mistake as she didn't want anyone inebriated, but fully alert for what might be coming.

The men sat on the floor, the six girls and Sally perched on the bed, she sat in solitary splendour on the one chair. They devoured the refreshments with relish and the mood, which had been sombre, was immediately improved.

There was nothing she could do apart from keep their spirits up and their minds off what might happen. The house was secure, reinforcements had been sent for, all they had to do was remain where they were, out of danger, until the men outside were captured, killed or fled.

The men took it in turns to keep an eye on things outside. The intruders brought the cart into the stable yard and then stood about as if expecting to be welcomed. One of them tried knocking on the back door and must obviously have walked around the house and seen that all the shutters were closed and the doors firmly bolted.

It was doubtful they would know about the cellar entrance, but if they did, again the door had been locked so they couldn't get into the house that way either. If there was one thing she didn't like it was sitting about doing nothing.

'I am going up into the attics to see if I can find anything that will help to make the house look festive. Girls, you come with me, each of you bring a candlestick. The rest of you must take it in turns to spy on the intruders. If anything changes out there you must come and fetch me at once.'

From the number of cobwebs, vermin droppings, and general grime she was certain nobody had visited the uppermost floor of this house for a decade at least. The girls huddled miserably behind her not enjoying this expedition at all.

'Put your candles somewhere safe where they cannot be knocked over. The last thing we want is to set fire to the house.' No sooner had she said the words than the thought slipped into her head that that this was the one thing the men outside could do. The house was solid, but oil-soaked rags, twigs and logs set against the doors would eventually ignite. Once the doors were burning it would only be a matter of time before it spread into the wooden panelling that ran through most of the ground floor.

She had no wish to alarm her reluctant helpers so looked around for something to occupy their attention. There was an assortment of discarded furniture which was of no interest to her, but at the far end underneath the window were three large, locked trunks.

'See, we must open these. There might be treasure inside. Think how pleased Lord Duval would be if we were to present him with a trunk full of gold and precious stones?'

This was nonsense, of course, but it was enough to gain their attention and their sullen mood lifted. Sally discovered a broken chair leg which she used to prise open the lock. The first lid was thrown back and it revealed nothing more interesting than documents, papers and ledgers. Disappointed, they attacked the second and this too held nothing exciting — merely handwritten books that were obviously diaries.

The third was more difficult to open and took the combined efforts of three maids to hammer open the padlock. When the lid crashed back there was a stunned silence.

'Are these real gold coins, miss?' Sally asked as she held one up to examine it.

Honour put her hand into the trunk and pulled a handful out. The gold was dull, and the coins had strange writing

116

on them, but she was certain they were genuine.

'I think these are Spanish doubloons, they could be two hundred years old. Far older than this house, so I wonder how they got here.'

Her musings were interrupted by the hideous sound of gunfire followed by screams and shouts. She dropped the gold she was holding into her pocket, slammed down the lid and gathered her little flock of terrified girls together.

'Quickly, pick up your candles, we must go down immediately. I need to see what is happening.' She wasn't sure if the gunshots had come from inside or outside.

7

Ralph knew he couldn't run flat out for a mile and still have enough breath to fight. The wound he had received in his side had punctured his lung. The physician who had sewn him up, and saved his life, nine months ago had told him so.

In order to conserve his energy he ran thirty paces and then jogged thirty and his orderly kept pace with him. The fact that his man kept glancing sideways meant Gifford was expecting him to keel over at any moment. This he would not do. Whatever the risks to his permanent recovery, he would not allow any men under his command to die today.

They were within sight of the outbuildings. 'Have your weapons ready, do not cock them, but they must be primed to fire.' He wasn't sure his makeshift band were capable of doing two things at once, but he and Gifford drew their pistols as they ran.

He raised his hand when they were near enough to be heard, and flattened himself against the wall of the stables. The sound of disgruntled voices was quite audible. Fitzroy's men had discovered they couldn't get in the house and were discussing what to do next.

Their ruse, of masquerading as the men returning with the greenery, had failed. He edged towards the corner, beckoned one of the armed men to accompany him. He then indicated that Gifford take the other end of the building with the remaining man. The four with only makeshift cudgels were to remain out of sight unless called for.

He had fought skirmishes against three times the number of his men, it was not the odds that bothered him but the fact only two of them were skilled in warfare. Surprise would have to be sufficient to win the day.

Gifford was waiting for his signal. Ralph beckoned to the nearest man.

'When we go you four must make as much racket as you can. Shout to each other as if you are a company of men about to strike.'

The young man looked perplexed. 'Not sure what that would be, my lord, I ain't no notion how soldiers behave.'

'Just shout, it doesn't matter what it is as long as you make enough noise to convince the men we are about to attack and that there are more of us than there are.'

The thing that worried him most was the fact that there could be as many as a dozen men waiting around the corner and all of them could be armed. He would make his two bullets count and then charge with his sword. It might not be enough to be successful, but it was the best he could do. The noise, the gunshots, should warn the two young men bringing the horses to stay away, which was the most important thing.

He returned to the corner and spoke to the shivering man, his pistol hanging slack by his side. 'It doesn't matter if you don't hit anyone with your bullet, just fire it and then get out of sight.'

After a steadying breath or two he raised his arm and dropped it. Simultaneously the four of them erupted around the corner and fired at the group of men standing by the horse and cart. His aim was true and two of the men screamed and collapsed clutching their chests. Gifford hit a third, but the other bullets thudded harmlessly into the wall. The yelling and screaming coming from behind him added to the chaos.

He drew his sword and was about to charge, giving the blood-curdling yell he had used as a soldier, when the docile mare, unused to gunfire and terrified by the noise, reared and bolted. Unable to get through the narrow archway that led towards the house she swerved sideways swinging the cart after her and by so doing managed to sweep half a dozen men from their feet.

Then the yard was suddenly full of riderless horses and the day was won. He had the opportunity to reload his

guns, as did Gifford, and he strode forward. 'Drop your weapons and surrender
if you want to live.' His voice carried
wonderfully and had the desired effect.
Those that were still on their feet did as
instructed and whilst he and Gifford
held them at gunpoint his other men
appeared.

Three would-be attackers were dead,
three had broken limbs, and the rest
were able to walk. 'Gifford, get the corpses
into a barn, take those unharmed into
the cellar and tie them up. The injured
can go into an empty stall . . . no, dammit.
There will be none free once we have
stabled their mounts.'

Then a side door opened and
Honour hurried out closely followed by
her erstwhile maid and two other girls.
'I say, my lord, that was capital. We have
come to take care of the injured.'

He was about to send her away but
then reconsidered. 'They are not coming
into the house. Where do you require
them to go?'

'The laundry room, it is warm enough

in there. We shall attend to them here first, they must not be moved until we've seen how bad their injuries are.'

Gradually the stable yard was being restored to order. The doors were opened and the extra horses were taken in. They were a mangy lot and he didn't want whatever infestations they might have to be passed onto his cattle.

'Make sure these animals are kept apart from mine. Desdemona and her pups must remain where they are — I'll not have them disturbed.'

The man he had addressed touched his cap and nodded. 'I reckon it'll mean putting some of these extras in the paddock with a rug on. There's not enough room in the stables.'

'Do the best you can. Make sure they have feed and water, there's the open barn where they can shelter if necessary.'

Honour and her maid were dealing with the injured men efficiently. It occurred to him that he had not asked her where they had gained the knowledge to do this, he had just assumed they would know. Two of the men had broken a leg but the third was merely nursing his arm.

'Miss Fitzroy, when you have patched that one up I shall interrogate him. Gifford will remain with you whilst you do it and then bring him to me.' He had raised his voice slightly so the villain could not fail to hear him. 'Bring him to the dairy. I have just to collect the items I shall need, and then I shall be ready for him.'

'Yes, my lord.' His orderly spoke to Honour directly but again for the benefit of the prisoner. 'The major's an expert in extracting information, miss, so don't mind the screams and such.'

She played along wonderfully. 'I've heard that pulling out fingernails is very effective. Also holding a person's head under water for several minutes works — but one has to be careful not to drown the suspect.'

Ralph turned away to hide his smile. He was an expert at interrogation but had never had to resort to such methods to learn what he wanted to know.

By the time he had inspected all the horses, his hounds, and found the rope he needed, Gifford was bringing the man with the damaged arm. He tossed the end over a beam and then hastily tied it into a hangman's noose. He left this dangling in plain sight.

'Shut the door, better that no one sees what goes on in here.'

Gifford pushed the shivering wretch towards the noose and then slipped it over his neck. He stood beside him with the other end around his waist and gripped firmly with both hands as if he was about to hoist the villain up.

'Who sent you?' Ralph snarled.

'I ain't stupid, I know I'll likely dangle in the end, but not now, your worship, if you please. Sir Edward Fitzroy paid us to snatch his cousin.'

'Go on, I am listening.'

'The toff said as we didn't 'ave to be too careful wiv 'er neither, if you gets me meaning?'

'Where were you to take her?'

'To 'is 'ouse, me lord, it ain't no more than a few hours from 'ere. One or two of the boys might 'ave wanted to 'ave 'urt 'er, but not me nor most of us. She wouldn't 'ave come to no 'arm if we 'ad got 'er.'

'How much were you paid?'

'I ain't sure, it weren't me what negotiated the price. We ain't 'ad nothing yet, that's for sure.'

Ralph came to a decision. 'Release him, Mr Gifford, if you please. Bring him along.' He turned to the wretch. 'I want you to identify the men who would have harmed Miss Fitzroy.'

The man seemed unbothered by this request — these were desperate times for men without employment and he had decided to be lenient with those that were merely trying to earn a few shillings to keep them alive through the winter. The others would not be so lucky.

He left Gifford to escort the prisoner and he hoped that the men who had died were those that deserved to. If they were not among the corpses then they would be handed over to the militia and no doubt be executed at the next assizes. The remainder he would feed, give a few shillings to each, and then send them on their way.

After all, it would soon be the season of goodwill to all men, he wanted to have no more deaths on his conscience. Sir Edward was another matter entirely and one he intended to deal with himself. He would like to break his neck, but then he would be the one that dangled, so he'd make sure the man was ruined socially and financially and then force him to go into exile.

★　★　★

Honour splinted the broken limbs and had crutches made for those that needed them. They were absurdly grateful, hardly the vicious villains she had thought they would be.

'You have fractures, not serious, and if you can manage to stay off that leg for a week or two it should heal and not leave you lame.'

'It won't make no never mind whether we can walk or not, miss, we'll be dead before Christmas,' the younger of the two said with a resigned sigh.

'You both seem like reasonable fellows, why risk your lives in this way?'

'Starving ain't pleasant, miss, 'specially not in the cold,' the other added morosely.

'How did you earn your living before you were involved in this business?'

'Jimmy and me worked on the land but was laid off weeks ago.'

'Why not go into the poorhouse? At least there you would have had shelter and food for the winter.'

'We ain't from round 'ere, miss, they wouldn't take us.'

She had sent two of the girls to fetch sacks from the granary and asked for four of them to be filled with straw. These two unfortunate men could sleep on them, and then use any spare as blankets.

Sally was now busy in the kitchen

preparing a giant stew as there were nine extra mouths to feed. Even if Ralph might say something to the contrary, she could not allow them to freeze or go hungry whatever they had been intending to do to her.

Gifford came back accompanied by the one with the broken arm who looked remarkably cheerful. 'They can remain in here for the moment, they can hardly be tied up in a barn as they are injured.'

'His lordship is only handing over two of the men to the authorities — the rest will be able to leave in the morning.'

The door opened and instead of Ralph's men coming in with the sacks, four of the would-be kidnappers came instead. She left Gifford to organise their temporary quarters and hastily retreated to the warmth of the house.

What had happened to Mr Ensley and the villagers? They had been supposed to come to their rescue, but were conspicuous by their absence. Her first concern was to remove her soiled garments, wash thoroughly and then she would be ready to speak to Ralph and hopefully have some answers.

Polly had everything waiting for her, even a jug of hot water which was a luxury she hadn't expected in the circumstances. When dressed, she scarcely noticed what was put on her, she was eager to go down and get some replies to the questions that were bothering her.

She headed for the small drawing room and was pleased to see Ralph was there before her. He jumped to his feet as she came in. 'I was about to go in search of you, there is much we have to talk about before we dine.'

'There is only one thing I want to know and that is, was it my cousin behind the attempted abduction as you thought?'

'It certainly was, but the majority of the men he hired are not out-and-out villains, just desperate and prepared to do anything.'

'The three I treated were certainly not vicious criminals. I am delighted that you have shown clemency, that you are going to let them go free in the morning.'

He sat and stretched out his long legs towards the fire. 'Actually, I have decided to keep them. Three of them are labourers, one a cowman, but the other three are tradespeople — a carpenter, a wheelwright and one skilled in brewing. All will be useful when I start to restore the house and re-enter Society.'

Then she understood. Once they were married he would have access to her massive fortune and could do as he pleased with it. 'Now that we have nothing to fear from my cousin the necessity for me to marry you has gone. I am sure that you agree, Ralph, that it would be extremely unwise to marry so hastily when we scarcely know each other. I fear you will have to postpone your plans.'

His eyes narrowed, he was no longer an amicable friend but a formidable stranger. 'You are wrong on all counts, my dear Honour. Fitzroy is a dangerous man and he will not abandon his nefarious plans just because he failed the first time.

'He will not try and take you, he will try and murder you. Which is another reason I have taken on those seven men; the house will need to be guarded at all times if you are to remain safe until your name day.'

'Are you suggesting that in order to keep me safe you must marry me?'

'I think you have misunderstood the situation. I have no more desire to become leg-shackled than you. I offered to do so thinking it was the only way I could protect you. Are you quite sure that Fitzroy cannot access your fortune after your death once you are of age?'

'Of course he can. Unless I write a will that leaves the money elsewhere and then send him a copy I cannot see there is anything we can do apart from get wed.'

'Then you must write one immediately and copy it. I will have it delivered to him tomorrow.' He turned the air blue and his language made her blush. 'We cannot do that, it will just make him the more determined to kill you before New Year's Day.'

'We appear to be going around in circles, my lord. Can you keep me safe without us being married for the next three weeks or can you not?'

He scowled into the fire and didn't answer. 'I am a soldier, you will be protected.' Then his face cleared and he smiled directly at her. The wave of heat that engulfed her quite took her by surprise.

'I intend to sell half my land. That way I will have sufficient funds to improve this property and to invest in a business venture.'

'Ralph, I have not had time to tell you of my discovery. I cannot believe we have been sitting here exchanging words about your finances when you are a fabulously rich man.' She delved into her reticule and tossed the five coins she had brought down with her into the air. They glinted in the firelight and his lightning reactions allowed him to reach out and catch all five in his palm.

'Where in God's name did you get these?'

'There is a chest full of them in the attic. I believe them to be Spanish doubloons — have you any idea how they came to be there?'

He was on his feet and grabbed her hand pulling her up to join him. 'Show me, I must see this miracle for myself.'

He handed her a candlestick and took one himself. The last thing she wanted was to go back into the dark, damp attic, but he had the right to see for himself that she wasn't telling Banbury tales.

It didn't seem quite so unpleasant with him beside her. He gave a cursory glance to the gold coins and was more interested in the documents in the other two trunks. 'This is fascinating stuff, I shall have it all brought down tomorrow and we shall read it together. I take it that you can read Spanish?'

'Not very well, I speak it, but am better versed in French and Italian.'

'I'm sure we will muddle through together. It will give us something to occupy our time as it will be safer for us to remain inside.'

They arrived as Cooper came in search of them to tell them dinner was served in the breakfast parlour. Tonight there was simple fare, but delicious nonetheless.

'This is the stew Sally was cooking in order to feed the extra mouths. It reminds me of the time I spent in the hills in Italy before my father died. Peasant food, but filling and very tasty.' She helped herself to another bowlful, and tore off a second chunk of freshly baked bread to dip into it. 'Sally learned to cook when we were travelling, I fear I shall not be able to persuade her to leave with me as she has always wanted to run a kitchen in a house like this.'

'I have not eaten so well for . . . well, for ever. I much appreciate the fact that you have given up your personal maid so that she can cook for us.'

'I have been thinking about our conversation earlier, I require to know how you intend to stop a would-be assassin from getting to me.'

8

Ralph had no intention of skulking inside waiting for whoever was sent by Fitzroy. However, what he planned to do was not something he intended to share with Honour. If he couldn't persuade the man to leave voluntarily, then he wouldn't hesitate to put him on the next ship to the colonies himself. This was something it would be better she did not know.

'There will be men patrolling the house and grounds day and night. As long as you stay away from the windows and do not go outside nothing untoward will happen.'

'As long as the shutters do not have to remain closed I shall be content. It would still be easier for me to leave and not put you to all this trouble.'

'Fitzroy cannot possibly be aware that his mission has failed. You are certainly at no risk from him at the moment.'

'What if he is close by?'

'Not according to the men I interrogated. Fate has thrown us together, sweetheart, and we have both benefited from this event. I should never have gone up into the attic and discovered the coins. If you had not been here they would have remained where they were. I am now fabulously wealthy and forever in your debt.'

'Fiddlesticks to that! You opened your house to me, put your life at risk for me, it is I that am in your debt.'

'Then we are even. I am at a loss to understand what happened to Ensley and the villagers, I shall investigate tomorrow. The militia also failed to appear — it is a puzzle I intend to solve at the earliest opportunity.'

'I am replete, after two helpings of stew and two slices of apple pie I could not eat another morsel. Do you intend to remain in here and drink port or are you coming to the drawing room with me?'

'I dislike port, sweet and sickly. I do

not drink alcohol at all as a general rule therefore, I shall come with you.'

'Now you have footmen, Ralph, I think you must have a livery made. They look incongruous opening and shutting doors and running errands dressed as they are.'

'As long as they do their work efficiently I care not what they look like. Do you play the pianoforte?'

She shook her head. 'Another feminine accomplishment I am not good at. I can play, but not well, would not do so in front of another. Neither can I paint a pretty picture or embroider a chair back.'

'As I have no intention of asking you to do any of those things, then you are safe from criticism. I, on the other hand, have a great fondness for music.' Her expression made him laugh. 'I might be a rough soldier, sweetheart, but I do have some redeeming features. Shall I play for you?'

'I should think the piano is sadly out of tune having been stored in that freezing cold music room for years.'

'Fear not, Miss Fitzroy, and take your seat in the drawing room.' He ushered her in and then picked up the violin case he had put in there earlier. 'I do play the piano but prefer this instrument as it is more portable.'

As always when he played he was soon lost in the melody. When the final notes faded he looked up to see her staring at him as if she had never seen him before.

'That was exquisite, Ralph. I am finding it hard to reconcile the two sides of your character. How can a man who makes his living by killing people also be a brilliant musician?'

'Being able to play an instrument is what keeps me sane — it also helps to settle my men to hear a lively jig before a battle.'

'From what little I know about your life I cannot see how you were able to become so expert on the violin.'

'My mother was married to my father by her parents. There was never any

140

love between them — I doubt there was even affection or respect, certainly not on her side. She kept me safe from the debauchery as best she could and she taught me to play. Before she died she sent me away to school and I was here as infrequently as possible.

'When I was fifteen years of age I joined the cavalry and have not visited Devil's Gate until this year.'

'It is fortuitous that you did as both our lives would be very different otherwise.'

There was a knock on the door and the tray with the coffee was brought in and placed on the central table. He waved the servant away and the door closed quietly behind him.

'I was wondering if we had sufficient provisions in the larders and stores to feed so many extra staff.'

'I have no idea, I leave such matters to Ensley.'

She was at the table pouring out the coffee and whilst she was engrossed in this task he had the opportunity to observe her without her knowledge. She wore her hair simply, gathered in a knot at the back of her head. It was a glorious golden colour and he would dearly like to see it loose and run his fingers through it.

She turned to bring the cups across. 'Do you remember the first thing I said to you?'

'I do indeed. You asked me to marry you.'

'I have never asked any woman such a question even in jest.'

'I shall not hold you to it, Ralph, we would be constantly at daggers drawn. Now that you are wealthy and intend to be part of the *ton* you will have dozens of hopeful mamas with marriageable daughters knocking at your door. No doubt you will find someone who would suit you better than I.'

He was about to make a light reply but instead spoke what was in his heart. 'I have met the woman I intend to spend the remainder of my life with and she is here in this very room with me right now.' He put down his cup so hard it disintegrated, but he ignored it.

Before she could respond, run away, he was standing in front of her blocking her passage. 'I know we have only known each other a few days, but I have fallen irrevocably in love with you.' He dropped to one knee and took her hands in his. They were soft, small in his, and they were trembling slightly.

'Miss Fitzroy, would you make me the happiest of men and become my wife?'

She removed her hands from his and his hopes were dashed. 'I cannot give you my answer now, my dear, but do not look so downcast, I have not refused the offer. If you would be prepared to wait, to ask me again after my anniversary, I will be ready to give you my decision.'

He stood up, feeling foolish after revealing his feelings when she did not reciprocate. 'You need to know me better? Is that why you hesitate?'

'Exactly so. I must be sure that the

connection we have is more than physical. I might be an innocent, Ralph, but I know that there is a difference between passion and romantic love. I could not marry without having both.'

'Do you have either?'

She became flustered under his intense scrutiny and he had his answer. They had passion but there was love only on one side. As far as he was concerned that was sufficient to make a good union, but he would never force the issue. She must come to a decision on her own. He had waited all his adult life to fall in love, so waiting for another three weeks was a mere bagatelle.

He offered his hand and after a second she took it. He gently pulled her to her feet and only just resisted the temptation to kiss her.

'Good night, sweetheart, I hope you will join me for breakfast and not have a tray in your room.'

'I look forward to it. I intend to visit the injured men first. Which reminds me, I hope everyone was fed and has sufficient covering to keep them warm tonight.'

'I'm going to visit the laundry room and the storeroom in which the prisoners are being held before I turn in.'

He escorted her to her apartment and then marched through the house and into his own rooms in order to put on his greatcoat and muffler before he went outside. Fortunately, someone had recovered it from the field where he had dropped it earlier.

Gifford was now his second-in-command, no longer serving as his valet. He was quite capable of taking care of himself when he had to. He had not posted guards tonight as Fitzroy would not have had time to discover why his first plan had failed.

Both the indoor and outside men had comfortable billets in the chambers set aside for that purpose when the house had been fully staffed. The new maids had quarters on the other side of the servants' hall which would mean that any fraternising would involve a long trek and hopefully this would discourage dalliances between them. The new men would join them there tomorrow.

What he didn't have was enough space in the stables to keep the twelve horses he had acquired today. That was something he would discuss with his estate manager when he eventually turned up. He was not unduly worried about his absence, the man was resourceful, he would have a good reason for not arriving.

Gifford was waiting for him by the side door that when opened would lead directly to the stable block. 'It's perishing out there, Major, I reckon we should bring in the new men and put the prisoners in the laundry if we don't want them to freeze to death.'

'I thought the same. I am going to check on my dogs and the horses. I shall leave the rest to you.'

★   ★   ★

146

Honour tumbled into bed her head full of inappropriate thoughts. When he looked at her in that particular way she could not think straight and wanted him to kiss her. She had never been kissed by a gentleman, young ladies did not indulge in such pastimes unless they wished to have no reputation left.

She stretched and plumped up the pillows before snuggling down to sleep. The last thing that filled her mind before she dozed off was — that as she had already destroyed her good name by living in a house without a chaperone with an unmarried gentleman — what did she have left to protect?

Something disturbed her slumber a few hours later. She didn't move, she was too comfortable for that, but she was alert and her eyes were open trying to fathom what had woken her up. The room was inky black, apart from the faintest glow from the dying fire. It was unpleasantly cold and the curtains that hung on either side of the bed were moving.

How could that be? Was that a creak from a floorboard? She held her breath. The hair on the back of her neck stood to attention. There it was again — she was not alone. The draughts must come from an open window through which the intruder had climbed.

Slowly she drew her knees up to her chin and then stood up. With one foot she pushed a pillow into the hollow she had made in the mattress, and then flicked the comforter back so it looked as if she was still sleeping there.

Another slight sound. The person was halfway across the room. The end of the bed was against the wall, but there was a gap of several inches. If she could somehow manage to get into that space, without alerting whoever it was, she would be safe from harm.

Her fingers were shaking. Finding the gap in the curtains was impossible. Could he hear her breathing? Her heart was pounding in her ears. Then her hands slid through and touched the wall. In one sinuous movement she stepped backwards over the bedhead and slithered into the small space.

There was more room than she had expected and she was able to shuffle sideways. If she could reach the window she could climb out, run around the house and bang on Ralph's door. The would-be assassin must be almost at the bed. She had to make a decision. Should she stay where she was and hope she would not be discovered or make a dash for freedom?

Without conscious thought she was moving, her bare feet making no sound on the boards, and dived headfirst through the open window. She landed on her hands and knees in the snow. Only then did it occur to her there might be others and they could be waiting right where she was.

Her eyes became accustomed to the darkness, the silvery light of the moon reflected on the snow making it easier to run without crashing into something. She fled along the frozen terrace, around the corner and towards the place where Ralph was sleeping.

The shutters were pulled tightly across, as they were in all the ground floor rooms. How had the intruder managed to open them and climb into her chamber so easily? She hammered on the glass and was about to scream his name when they flew back, the window was thrown up and she was snatched from her feet and lifted to safety.

Her teeth were chattering. She was frozen to the marrow. He didn't ask why she was there, he carried her to his bed, dropped her in, then pulled over the covers so she was snug. His warmth lingered on the sheets. She recovered the power of speech.

'There's someone in my room. I managed to get out of the window he had left open. I don't know if there are more than one of them.'

By the time she had finished speaking he had pulled on his breeches and boots. Then he swirled his greatcoat around his shoulders and was ready to leave. 'Close the window and lock the shutters after me. Then return to my bed and try and get warm.'

Then he was gone. She tumbled out and staggered across to do as he said. Her feet were numb, making it difficult to walk without falling. He had said get into the bed but she was so cold she needed a fire to warm the room.

Slowly she made her way to the grate and pushed a candle into the embers. Once this was alight she looked round for something to use as kindling. There was nothing in the bedchamber, but there might well be in his sitting room.

She made her way with difficulty into this room — it was almost as cold as outdoors. There was a desk on the far side of the room and there was bound to be paper of some sort in it. She was halfway across when a strange lethargy overcame her. She would feel so much better if she slept. Her legs buckled beneath her and she crumpled to the carpet and knew no more.

Ralph didn't run. He kept himself close to the wall. His muffler was around his face so only his eyes were visible. In his dark coat it was unlikely anyone would see him. Then he increased his pace to a flat run as he saw a figure emerging from the window. His pistol was in his hand, cocked and ready to fire without him having to think about it.

He didn't shout a warning. He stopped, raised the gun and slowly squeezed the trigger. The sound of the shot echoed into the night but the scream of the man as he fell was even louder. He pushed the shape with his boot but there was no response.

He cursed under his breath. His beloved girl could have been dead and it would have been his fault. How could Fitzroy have got someone here so quickly? And more importantly, how did they know which rooms to enter? Bile rose in his throat. There was only one explanation.

Gifford arrived at a run and was holding a wildly swinging lantern in one hand and a pistol in the other. 'Hold that still whilst I look at the body. God's teeth! One of the men from the laundry room.'

'I was just there, Major, I saw no sign of an escape. How the hell did he get free?'

'You're missing the point, Gifford. Someone we thought loyal to us released them and told them which room was Honour's. I hope to God we have not been duped, as they are now inside and have access to all parts of the house.'

'Whoever it is will have heard what happened, Major, we'll not surprise them this time.'

'Let us go in through this window, lock it behind us. I don't give a damn what's going on outside. I need to know that Honour is safe.'

His orderly secreted the lantern behind the skirt of his greatcoat so it couldn't be seen by anyone they were approaching but would give them just enough light to find their way through the house. They checked that each window and door was still locked and they all were.

'Either someone went out and then came in again, or the men in the laundry room got free by themselves. But this doesn't explain how they knew which window to prise up.'

They were now outside his own apartment, he quietly pushed open the bedchamber door and listened. All quiet. He could now concentrate on discovering if they were seeking one man or several. He had returned his sword to the armoury but had both his pistols. They had been reloaded and were ready to fire if necessary.

'Exactly where are the new arrivals sleeping?'

'In a room next to our own men.'

'I'll investigate there, you rouse the others. We might need their assistance if all those I showed mercy to prove to be dissembling.'

He was unfamiliar with this side of the house as he rarely went down to the servants' quarters, but Gifford's instructions were clear and he found the chamber he was seeking with no difficulty. He stood outside the door uncertain how to proceed. Was he dealing with a cunning adversary who would pretend to be a loyal man until he could achieve his aims? If this was the case the culprit would already be back in his bed and there would be no evidence that he had ever left.

On the other hand, they could all be perfectly innocent of any further wrongdoing and the attack had been solely the work of the two he already knew were true villains. He needed to catch the accomplice and force him to talk, to tell him how they knew which window belonged to Honour.

This door must be blocked so nobody could get out until he knew the truth. Fortunately, the door opened outwards so all that was needed was a large piece of furniture and they would be held captive. The windows on these subterranean chambers were small, a grown man could not wriggle through one even if he wanted to.

He turned as there was a faint noise behind him and Gifford and half a dozen men, their garments pulled on hurriedly over their nightclothes, joined him. He explained what he wanted and in minutes a heavy oak sideboard was pushed hard against the door making sure it could not be opened from the inside.

'We shall exit through the cellars, Gifford, you and three others come with me, the rest of you remain on guard outside my apartment. Make sure the door is locked behind us as before.'

Although they had moved the furniture as quietly as possible the noise might well have woken up those inside the chamber. The innocent would be puzzled as to why they were barricaded into the room, but if anyone was guilty they would understand at once they would be unmasked in due course.

He was unsurprised when Sally appeared fully dressed. He quickly explained what was going on.

'I shall go to Miss Fitzroy, she will need hot bricks and a fire immediately.'

The girl vanished, the candle flickering as she hurried away.

9

Honour could hear someone calling her name, but it was faint, and she was so tired she did not have the energy to wake and answer this insistent voice.

'Miss Fitzroy, drink this, you will feel better when you're warm.'

Reluctantly she forced her heavy eyelids up and saw Sally looking down at her. Before she could protest, hot, spiced wine was tipped into her mouth and she had no option but to swallow it. After the first mouthful she began to feel more awake and eagerly drank the rest.

The room was ablaze with candle-light, a huge fire burned in the grate, but she had no idea exactly where she was or why Sally was taking care of her and not her new maid. She looked around and slowly recognition came to her. This was Ralph's domain and she was in his bed in her nightgown, but swathed in red flannel so she could barely move.

'What am I doing in this chamber? I have no recollection of coming here.'

'Someone tried to murder you, miss, and you escaped through your bedroom window and came here for help.'

Then what had happened flooded back and she began to shake. Her teeth chattered against the silver mug and Sally hastily took it from her hands. Then she was tucked up like a small child and allowed to fall asleep again. Her last waking thoughts were that Ralph would have to sleep in her chamber as he could hardly remain in here with her.

★   ★   ★

'Major, did you look inside the room and see if all the beds were occupied?' Gifford asked.

Ralph's stomach clenched as he understood the significance of this question.

159

'It would only need one person to return in order to lock the doors and the remainder could still be outside. Tarnation take it! Before my injury I would not have made such an error of judgement.'

'I'll check for you, sir, no need for you to be involved.'

Ralph moved from the door so the sideboard could be dragged away and the door opened. Gifford stood to one side and pushed the door open so violently it smashed against the wall. If they had not been awake before, they would be so now.

His man held up the lantern and did a rapid headcount. He then stepped aside, the door was closed and the sideboard returned. This was completed without a word being spoken.

'All present and correct, Major. There can be only one man outside the house.'

There were grumbles and raised voices coming from inside the room but nobody attempted to open the door. They must realise why they had been shut in and were resigned to the fact that they were not trusted.

The cellars were icy, but here was the best place to discuss his tactics as they could not be overheard by anyone.

'The stables are locked so he cannot steal a horse and escape. I doubt he will be attempting a second attack now that he knows we are looking for him. Be careful, he could be armed, but I doubt it.'

'Gifford take those two and search the outbuildings from that side. I shall do the same from the other. We will reconnect in the stable yard.'

It was marginally warmer outside. He led the men onto the track and they separated as he had instructed. One of the men also had a lantern beneath his coat. They moved silently from place to place, the only sound the crunching of their boots in the snow. He must examine the storeroom thoroughly where the prisoners had been locked up.

'Over here, my lord. I've found the ropes and they've been cut through clean as a whistle,' one of the men said quietly.

The door had been unbolted not kicked open, this confirmed that at least one of the men inside had helped them. It would have been easy enough to take knives from the kitchen — this meant that whoever he was searching for was armed, but only with a knife as there had been nothing removed from the armoury when he had checked.

They continued to search every store, barn and shed to no avail. Where the devil was this man? Gifford had had no better success than him.

'Were there any horses missing from the paddock?'

'No, Major, I just checked. He has to be somewhere close by waiting for his accomplice to act.'

'We cannot remain out here much longer as only you and I are properly dressed. We shall have to resume the search tomorrow morning when we will have more chance of seeing any evidence left behind. This will mean that those men must remain where they are for the moment.'

With some relief he led them back to the side door and gave the agreed knock. Immediately it was opened and they were back in the warm.

'There is one possibility we haven't considered — that the second man is inside the house already. I think he will have hidden upstairs, so I should like two men to guard each staircase, two outside my apartment and then you and I will patrol the passageways. Get pistols from the armoury.'

'Miss Fitzroy will be well protected, my lord. There's no need for you to stay awake. If you don't mind me saying so, you don't look too clever. Get some shut-eye, I'll take care of things.'

Ralph was about to refuse, but his man was right, he was exhausted. 'I shall sleep in Honour's room. Fetch me if anything occurs.'

His legs were leaden, he was not as fit as he had thought. In fact, he doubted if he would ever be able to return to the regiment and fight alongside his men again. He would not be able to sleep until he was certain Honour was well after her unpleasant experience.

He forced his limbs to obey his command and knocked on his own bedroom door. It opened immediately. 'Is she well?'

'I found Miss Fitzroy unconscious on the floor of your sitting room. She was blue with cold, if she had remained there any longer she would have perished.'

His fatigue fell away and he charged across the room to his bed. His beloved girl was a little pale, but her skin was warm and she was sleeping peacefully. He turned to leave, but his legs almost gave way beneath him.

'No, my lord, you stop here where it's warm. There's plenty of room for both of you.'

He should have protested, but the girl was most insistent and guided him to the other side and then gently pushed him down. He flopped back too exhausted to argue. His boots were removed and then a warm comforter was draped over him.

Somehow he managed to push himself up on his elbows. 'I cannot sleep here, it will not do you know . . . '

'Never you mind that, my lord, I'll be sleeping in the chair by the fire and Polly will be right with me. No rules are being broken tonight.'

He flopped back and was instantly asleep.

$\star \quad \star \quad \star$

Honour woke again and for a moment was disorientated. There was something heavy resting across her waist. Good heavens! Ralph was beside her and so sound asleep even pinching his arm failed to wake him.

She had an urgent need and there was so much red flannel about her limbs she could not free herself. She feared there would be an embarrassing accident. She attempted to roll out but something was trapping her.

'Here, sweetheart, allow me to assist you.'

He was wide awake and carefully peeled back the layers that were restricting her movement until she was able to wriggle out. She was now standing in front of a gentleman in nothing more than her nightgown and had an urgent need to use the commode. She would rather die than do so in front of him.

There were two candles burning on the mantelshelf and the fire was still bright enough to add to the illumination of the room. She shifted from one foot to the other not sure what to do.

His laugh only added to her discomfort. Then he was beside her draping his silk bedrobe over her shoulders. 'What you need is behind that screen, I shall absent myself until you are done.'

He strolled away as if this was the most ordinary thing in the world. It was all very well for him, he was fully clothed apart from a lack of boots. She dashed to the screen and when she was done she tied the belt of the overlarge garment more securely and rolled up the sleeves so her hands were visible.

She remembered that Sally and Polly had been in the room earlier — why were they not here now as chaperones? The sitting room was also warm and welcoming, he had already lit several candles. He turned and she couldn't keep back her laugh.

'My word! That is not a shirt but your nightwear.'

'It is indeed, my love, I did not have time to dress correctly. I apologise for the fact that you woke to find yourself in a compromising position. Sally and your maid should have remained with us all night.'

'Did you catch the man who came into my room to kill me?'

'I did. However, there are several things I need to tell you and you had better sit down as none of them are pleasant.'

★   ★   ★

When he had done she nodded, but did not look particularly upset. She was a remarkable young lady — the more he saw of her, the more determined he was to persuade her to marry him. Had they been left alone deliberately in order to precipitate matters?

She jumped to her feet, her eyes wide. 'I heard something. Is it that another intruder?'

He waved her back to the *chaise longue*. 'No, I believe it is our breakfast coming. I wondered where the girls had gone.'

'I should not be sitting here dressed as I am, in your apartment, eating breakfast. It is most unseemly.'

'No one else will know, apart from our staff, unless you care to broadcast it about the place.'

She was saved from making an unwise reply as Sally and Polly arrived with laden trays. He heard her stomach rumble.

'I do beg your pardon. I am amazed that I am hungry after such an eventful night. A more delicately bred young lady would be swooning and demanding weak tea and dry toast.'

They were interrupted by her maid. 'My lord, I have put out your clothes and shaving things in your dressing room. I have Miss Fitzroy's garments ready. Do you intend to eat before or after you dress?'

For a maid, however senior, this girl was remarkably forthright. In fact, she was the female counterpart of his own Gifford.

'We shall dress, neither of us are comfortable as we are. Have the men begun the search of the upper floors?'

'Not only have they done that, my lord, they have caught the varmint. Mr Gifford has him trussed up like a Christmas goose and is about to ask him some questions.'

'Where is he, do you know?'

'He was about to take him to the laundry room, my lord.'

'I must join him immediately. Forgive me, sweetheart, duty calls.'

169

He dressed, didn't bother about shaving, and was out of the house and around to the outbuildings in record time. The two men standing guard nodded at his approach and stood aside.

The captive was suspended from the noose, but this time it was tight enough to cause him difficulty breathing. His orderly saluted.

'I thought I would save you the trouble, Major, and just hang the blighter now. The other one's dead so he might as well join him and save the militia a wasted journey.'

'A moment, Gifford, if you please. If he can give me the answer I require perhaps we can spare him. There is a message that must be delivered to his master and I might consider sending him.'

The man was now on tiptoes, almost dangling from the rope. He raised his head and Ralph saw a flicker of hope in his eyes. Excellent — he was ready to talk.

'How many of the men inside are

your accomplices?'

'Just the one, me lord. Billy Smith, the cockeyed one, he's me cousin. The others ain't part of it, they only took the job because they was starving.'

'Release him, but tie him securely and put him back in the storeroom. Place a guard outside.'

He returned at the speed with which he had exited and the two men guarding the door dragged the sideboard away. He flung it open and drawing himself up to his impressive height he stood in the doorway, glowering at the occupants.

They were all dressed and waited patiently for what was to come. He fixed each in turn with an icy stare — all but one returned his gaze.

'Bring Smith to me.'

Instantly the men nearest to the villain grabbed his arms. The wretch didn't struggle and allowed himself to be dragged across the room.

'Take him to Mr Gifford.'

His expression changed and he nodded at the remaining men. 'I apologise for having incarcerated you, but I could not be sure how many of you were part of the plot to murder my betrothed.'

They nodded and smiled, their relief obvious. 'We never knew Billy was with them, my lord, or we'd have done him in ourselves.'

'I need two of you to work in the stables whilst we have so many horses to take care of. The rest of you will patrol the grounds until I have had time to deal with Sir Edward.'

Ralph scarcely had time to draw breath before he was told that the militia had arrived, accompanied by Ensley.

'Have the officer escorted to my study along with Ensley,' he told Cooper.

They had both better have a good excuse for failing to appear yesterday when they were so desperately needed. He would not offer them refreshments. This would be a formal meeting.

At times like this he regretted that he was not in uniform, nobody argued with a major. The two men were escorted to his study and he remained in front of his desk, ramrod straight, his expression grim. There was an uncomfortable silence which he had no intention of breaking.

Ensley cleared his throat nervously. 'I gather that the matter has been dealt with satisfactorily. I must apologise for failing to arrive with reinforcements. I didn't reach the village yesterday, I suffered a fall from my horse and only by a stroke of good fortune was not left outside to freeze to death.

'I was taken unconscious to the Rectory and did not recover my senses until this morning. I am still not too steady on my feet.'

In two strides he was beside his factor, took his arm and guided him swiftly to the nearest chair. He then noticed the livid bruise down the side of his face which he had been too angry to see initially. 'Thank God you were found. I could not do without your able assistance. You should have sent a message, not come yourself when you are still so unwell.'

'I shall return to my own bed, if you will allow me to, my lord.'

The man was in no state to ride across the country. As always, he ignored the bell-strap and yelled through the door that someone come at once.

'Mr Ensley has a concussion; have a chamber prepared for him at once. He will be remaining here until he is recovered.'

Next, he turned his attention to the militia lieutenant. 'And what excuse have you for not coming to my aid?' He spoke to him as he would a junior officer and the man responded by standing to attention before he spoke.

'We had been called out to a disturbance some distance away and by the time we received your request it was too late to travel.'

Ralph quickly explained what had transpired and that there was one prisoner to be removed. 'I am going to see Sir Edward Fitzroy today.' There was no need to elaborate, both gentlemen were well aware that the matter would be settled one way or another before the day was out.

'If the men involved are prepared to swear an oath that they were recruited and paid by Fitzroy then he too can be arrested.'

'That will not be necessary. He will be leaving the country permanently which is punishment enough.'

The lieutenant saluted and marched smartly away to collect the single prisoner. Ensley was slumped in the chair barely conscious. The sooner he was safely in a warm bed the better.

★ ★ ★

Honour needed something to occupy her time. She must not dwell on what had happened, she must concentrate on something more pleasant. There was one thing she could do and that was start making garlands and wreaths to decorate the house.

It would be icy in the flower room — in fact, the greenery was very likely still outside on the cart. Therefore, this would be her first task. She would find some men to bring it in for her. She had yet to find any ribbons or lengths of material that could be used to make bows, this would be something else she could do.

She sent her maid to discover exactly where the ivy, holly and fir branches were. The girl was back in a state of agitation.

'The park is full of soldiers on horseback, miss, ever so handsome and smart they are. I'd have liked to have seen them when they were closer. They are leaving now.'

'They are none of your business, my girl. Did you discover the whereabouts of my greenery?'

'The cart isn't anywhere to be seen, miss. No one knows where it is and they weren't too interested in looking neither.'

This would not do at all. She would go in search of it herself. She had been told to remain inside, but the danger was now over so she could go out with impunity. With her cloak wrapped around her and her warmest gown underneath she would not suffer from the elements.

She used the side door as she had no intention of becoming embroiled with the militia. There were no outside men to ask about the missing items. There was no need to drag them away from their work. It should not be difficult to discover the whereabouts of something as large as a diligence.

The first place she would look would be the barn used for carts and other vehicles. As far as she was aware Ralph did not own a carriage. This was something else she must look into — she could not leave, if that was what she chose to do, until she had her own returned to her.

It was hard to comprehend that a few short hours ago there had been mayhem and murder out here as now it was quiet and well ordered, as it should be. The sky was clear of clouds, the sun bright and reflecting on the snow making everything look magical.

Since she had been here she had had no opportunity to explore the grounds. She would do so now. Desdemona, abandoning her litter for the moment, loped up and greeted her affectionately.

'I am going to look at the kitchen garden, and then continue my search for the greenery. Are you coming with me, girl?'

The dog wagged her tail as if understanding what was said to her. The kitchen garden was quite splendid, and then she went in search of the orangery. Inside this glass structure was an ingenious arrangement of pipes and glass and the interior was delightfully warm. The heady scent of orange and lemon blossom filled the air and everywhere she looked there were interesting plants growing. Was it possible they had a pineapple plant somewhere?

After spending a pleasant time in there the dog returned to her puppies and she resolved to continue her search for the diligence. As she stepped out she was grabbed from behind and a hand was placed over her mouth. Her bladder almost emptied so shocked was she.

She breathed in through her nose and her fear turned to fury. This was no villain, but Ralph who had for some reason best known to himself decided to terrify her.

Two could play at that game. She went limp and closed her eyes as if in a swoon. She had expected to be caught, to be apologised to, to be fussed over, but he just removed his grip and let her fall into the snow.

'I should not remain down there, sweetheart, you will get unpleasantly cold.'

She glared up at him, then held out her hand imperiously. He ignored it, turned his back and strolled away whistling.

He would pay for his behaviour. She turned onto her knees and quickly made herself a large, ice-packed snowball and hurled it at him. It burst with a satisfying thump on the back of his head making him stumble forward.

She knew him well enough to know he would not let this pass without retribution. Hastily, she gathered up further ammunition and began to hurl them with commendable accuracy hoping to drive him around the corner so she could make good her escape.

Instead he scooped up two large handfuls of snow, turned and threw them at her head. She had been expecting this and was able to sway sideways and let them pass harmlessly by. She laughed triumphantly and made herself two more missiles.

She had expected him to do the same but to her horror he raced towards her using his weight to carry her backwards so she was pinned against the wall.

'Are you declaring war on me, my love? You will not win. I am a military man.'

'You are a nincompoop and you are squashing me. Remove yourself at once.' He was laughing down at her and her arms moved of their own volition to link around his neck.

He needed no further encouragement and for a blissful few minutes she was lost to the world. Eventually he raised his head, his eyes blazing, his cheeks flushed.

'I love you, and I am determined to marry you whatever you think about the matter. I have already contacted the curate so when Fred returns with the special licence we can tie the knot.'

'How can we possibly commit ourselves to a lifetime together when we have only known each other so short a time?'

'Do you love me?'

'You know that I do.'

'Then I cannot see there is any reason not to get married. Waiting will not make us love each other less, but more, so why make ourselves miserable for no reason?'

He moved away sufficiently for her to take her revenge. She kicked him hard in the shins and he said something most impolite and then laughed.

'I deserved that, but in my defence, you should not have been creeping about the place on your own. I was merely pointing out to you how vulnerable you are.'

'The only danger to my person is you. I thought you were going to see my cousin? You would be better doing that than attacking your future wife.'

'I am going, but I thought that you might like to accompany me. Now that we are officially betrothed he cannot touch you and I can act on your behalf.'

'I am assuming that you don't intend to run him through in front of me.'

He chuckled and kissed her again. 'I should like to, but instead he will lose his estates, his reputation and be forced to live abroad for the rest of his life.'

'That sounds quite satisfactory. What about his son? He is a weak man, but would have been complicit in all this.'

'Good God! Of course, he will be going too. I shall take over his land and put in a tenant. It will do very nicely for our second son.'

'We are not even married and yet you are talking blithely of sons.'

'I shall be quite content if we have daughters as well.'

'I should like a large family but not everyone is blessed with children.'

'Very true, darling girl, but I intend to be assiduous in my attentions and it will not be from lack of trying if we remain childless.'

'How indelicate of you to mention such a thing. How long will it take, do you think, for Fred to return with the necessary documentation?'

'You will be Lady Duval before Christmas.'

They were now almost at the house. She stood on tiptoe and whispered in his ear. 'Then I see no obstacle to us being intimate immediately.' She had meant that night, but he took her literally.

He snatched her up and raced through the house, much to the astonishment of the servants, and deposited her on his bed.

* * *

The visit to Sir Edward did not take place until the following day as neither Honour nor Ralph emerged from the bedchamber until then.

We do hope that you have enjoyed reading this large print book.

Did you know that all of our titles are available for purchase?

We publish a wide range of high quality large print books including:
Romances, Mysteries, Classics
General Fiction
Non Fiction and Westerns

Special interest titles available in large print are:
The Little Oxford Dictionary
Music Book, Song Book
Hymn Book, Service Book

Also available from us courtesy of Oxford University Press:
Young Readers' Dictionary
(large print edition)
Young Readers' Thesaurus
(large print edition)

For further information or a free brochure, please contact us at:
Ulverscroft Large Print Books Ltd.,
The Green, Bradgate Road, Anstey,
Leicester, LE7 7FU, England.
Tel: (00 44) **0116 236 4325**
Fax: (00 44) **0116 234 0205**